ABOUT THIS BOOK

She's been the oracle for less than a month and she's already angered the gods. If she doesn't meet fate's demand, all of Havenwood Falls will suffer.

Lana Velis always knew she might one day inherit the powers and duties of the Oracle of Delphi, but the inheritance arriving in the middle of her last-ever college final wasn't something even she could predict.

With a power she never wanted and her testy cat, Lana must leave her best friend behind and make her way to Havenwood Falls to take over the never-ending petitioner list her ya-ya left behind. If only it were that easy. Now, not only is she saddled with a guardian she has no interest in having, but she's also forced to live with him.

And the hurdles keep coming. First, Lana must convince the Court of the Sun and the Moon to honor her title as the sacred oracle. Then she's bound by the laws of the gods to never tell someone's future if they aren't on her list—a law she struggles with, especially when she sees the unfathomable future of a little boy.

Now the gods are angry, and the Fates demand a soul in place of the one she stole—or all of Havenwood Falls will suffer the consequences. Lana must choose a soul to sacrifice, because in the end, Fate will always get its due.

HAVENWOOD FALLS BOOKS

Forever Loyal by E.J. Fechenda

Fate's Demand by Emily Cyr

The Wu & the Wand by T.V. Hahn

A Demon's Redemption by JD Nelson

Also try the YA line, Havenwood Falls High; the historical paranormal line, Legends of Havenwood Falls; the darker, sexier side of town, Havenwood Falls Sin & Silk; and the local supernatural college, Sun & Moon Academy.

Stay up to date at www.HavenwoodFalls.com

BOOKS BY EMILY CYR

The Lightning Witch Trilogy:

The Lightning Prophecy
The Lightning Legacy
The Lightning Progeny

The Vampire Favors Series:

Push and Pull

Give and Take

Fight or Flight

Sink or Swim

Stand-alone books:

Hotline to Hell

Mended

Blackened Magic

Coming soon:

The Lone Wolf

Back and Forth

FATE'S DEMAND

A HAVENWOOD FALLS NOVELLA

EMILY CYR

For Jess. Everyone needs a Jess in their life.
I'm glad I have mine.

CHAPTER 1

The way her short silver hair kissed that slim neck of hers sent chills throughout my whole body. That neck I'd spent two years loving, spent two years brushing my lips against. Now? Just what was I supposed to do? I was expected to just pick up the remnants of my shattered heart and move the hell on. How could anyone be expected to do that?

She knew I was there. I could tell by the way she hung all over the other woman. The one I'd caught her with. I was so stupid for still loving her, but apparently, she'd moved on long ago.

"Lana. You can't keep doing this to yourself." It was Jensen chiding me. It was always Jensen. Her kind voice had always been a balm to my soul, ever since we were kids. Now, here we were only a few finals until we graduated from college. She with a degree in education and I in graphic design. But as it was, none of that mattered, not when my heart had been so viciously ripped out.

"Earth to Lana," she prodded again. This time I glanced at her. She looked so much like the child she used to be, I couldn't help but smile at her. Her light brown skin was such a contrast to her vivid green eyes. Her spiraled ringlet curls hung around her face, making her rounded features stand out even more. She was beautiful. I was always so jealous of her. She stood at a whopping five foot seven, whereas I was five foot two on a good day. My skin seemed so pale in comparison to her richly tanned color, even though my Greek heritage gave me an olive complexion. However, she always said I never appreciated my pin-straight dark brown hair. She was right, as usual. My eyes were always my favorite feature. They were a bright blue and against my dark hair they stood out even more.

I sighed. "I know, it's just, I—" I choked on the words.

Jensen held up a slender hand in a stopping gesture. Her brow and lips tilted up slightly, causing her features to soften slightly. "I know you do. But you deserve better, girl."

Of course, she was right. "I know." There wasn't a whole lot more I could say.

"Come on, we have a final to get to. Did you even study? Greek history—shouldn't you be an expert? You being Greek and all?"

Glancing down at my phone, I realized she was correct. It was the only class the three of us shared, so it wasn't like it would be awkward or anything.

"Fuck no!" I exclaimed. I tried like hell to recall the last semester's worth of Greek history. "What were the three Fates' names again?" I blurted.

"Girl, if I have to tell you that, you're totally screwed." She laughed, shaking her head.

We walked to class as we always did, her trying to make me laugh, me brooding while trying like hell to remember the Fates' names and everything else I needed for that damn exam.

"So, what? Are you going to go back to dudes now?"

Her question caused me to choke on my own saliva.

Half coughing and half laughing, I looked at her and explained, "That's not really how it works. I'm bi. I kinda just love who I love."

"I know it's not, but I heard a laugh or two around that cock you were choking on just now, so hashtag worth it." Her crazy ass seemed to preen as her face lit up.

"You're the most inappropriate person I know." I laughed, rolling my eyes at her.

"Oh, that's so not true. You've met my mother."

"You win!" I cackled as we rounded the corner and walked into class.

This was it. My last final I'd have to take before real life would come crashing down on me.

We made our way to our seats and got settled in. My phone buzzed, and I looked down to see the text.

It was from my dad. Like I'd done for the last five years, I hit ignore. The absolute last thing I needed right then was my alcoholic father hitting me up for yet more money.

"Let me guess, your dad or ya-ya? Still letting them walk all over you?" It was her. My whole body froze at her words, not because of what she said but because of who had said it.

"Don't you have a rock to find, Cassidy?" Jensen taunted in a venom-laced tone.

Cassie looked at her in confusion.

"What?" Cassie spat. Her eyes were laser focused on Jensen.

"Oh, you know, the rock you crawled out from under and need to return to?" I heard several shocked inhalations of breath from around me at Jensen's dig.

I swear to Hades's bouncing balls my jaw hit the fucking tile floor with an audible clack.

The look of shock and hurt flashed so fast across Cassie's face, I questioned if I'd seen anything at all.

"See, this is why I found something better. You're no better than the company you keep. Remember that, Lana." She was so condescending. Come to think of it, she'd always been like that, not just to Jensen but to me as well. And her words were nothing more than a slap in the face meant to hurt me and Jensen. Then, under her breath, she said the words I thought I would never hear from someone I'd once loved: "No wonder your dad's an alcoholic."

I was so shocked I just sat there for a heartbeat. Then rage took over, and I stood to face her eye to eye. I'd had enough. Not because I actually cared about my father, but for the sheer fact that she had the gall to blame me for something I'd always blamed myself for—

something she'd known. She had the audacity to use my own insecurities against me? Yeah, fuck that.

"You know, Cassie, as I recall, I broke up with you. And, as I recall, you were trying to sext me, what, just last night? So really, who's the lucky one?"

She opened her mouth to speak, but fuck that. I wasn't having it.

"So, you want to give me advice?" I continued. "How about I give you some? You are what you eat."

The whole class was listening, including the TA and professor. I should have cared about the audience. But for once, I didn't care whom I offended or who heard my dirty laundry.

"What?" she said dumbly. Looking around for a split second, I saw the same look on nearly everyone's face.

Smiling my very best *eat shit and die* expression, I intoned, "You are what you eat. Me? I last ate a bagel. What did you eat? A rotting, stinking pus—" The world tilted and went black. But not before I saw Cassie's horrified expression. I couldn't help but laugh. Well, at least I thought I did.

CHAPTER 2

"*There must always be an oracle.*" The words swirled around me like a physical haze, something that could be heard but never touched.

Voices broke through the darkness like the lapping waves of a lazy ocean. My body felt fuzzy, as if my whole nervous system were replaced with a live wire. I felt like electricity was being pumped through my veins.

"What—" I tried to speak, but only a garbled sound came out.

"You fucking sack of dog shit!" Jensen screeched so loud, I honestly thought she was a pissed off parrot rather than her joyful self. *Is she yelling? Of course she is.*

"Hi." This time, while it felt and sounded garbled, the word was at least clear. Well, clearer.

Raising my hand to my throbbing head, I felt my forearm catch on something. Glancing down, I saw just what kept my hand from reaching my face—an IV. *What the hell?* It was only then that I took stock of where I was, in a hospital if the beeping monitors and machine-operated bed had anything to say about it.

"What the hell happened?" I croaked. I was so confused.

"How much do you remember?" Jensen inquired as she nibbled her bottom lip. Her obvious nervousness caused me to worry.

I tried to think back to the last thing I could remember, but every time I did, a massive headache would slam into me with the force of a damn Mack truck.

"Um, I remember going in for our final, then Cassie being a dick. Then—" I groaned as pain spiked in my head. "Nothing," I rasped.

Jensen shook her head, walked over to the bed, and sat down on the not-so-comfortable mattress. Her green eyes searched my face as her lips went from a soft smile to a worried line. Whatever it was, it was bad.

She took in a deep breath and explained. "You told Cassie off, which by the way, was epic. You should have seen her face when you said she was what she ate. Priceless." Her mouth turned into a slight smile, but then she looked at me fully and her smile dropped.

"Then you just dropped to the ground and started having a seizure. Do you have epilepsy? I didn't think you did, but I mean I—"

My eyes went wide as I blurted, "Wait, what? I had a what?"

There was no good goddamn way I'd heard her correctly.

"Uh, um, maybe the doctor should come and talk to you?" she suggested, looking from me to the door and back again.

"Also, um, your dad has been calling you, like, a lot," she added as she walked to the head of my bed.

"Wonderful. Sounds like a cherry on the shit sundae." I groaned.

She reached out to cup my face, a thing she'd done only four million times in our lives. But this time, as soon as her skin touched mine, white-hot pain shot through me like I'd been struck by lightning, or what I thought equated to such a thing. My whole body glowed with a bright white light, though that didn't scare me. It wasn't until I saw Jensen that I realized just what had happened.

I saw Jensen, but it wasn't her. I mean, it was, but it wasn't. I could see Jensen, the one I knew and loved, but there was another version of her. Time—well, the time I knew—seemed to slow to a near stop as the scene played out in front of me. It was like there was a hologram of her in the background of what I knew was real.

She is in a stunning white dress that hugs her slim body, then flares out at the bottom. Her image in the mirror and the smile on her face are so

6

real I can feel them in my heart. I can feel her feelings and hear her thoughts.

"Jensen!" her mother called, causing her to turn from the mirror.

"I know. It's time. Just give me a second!" she calls back, returning her attention to her reflection. "Please don't be a mistake," she whispers to no one, though deep down in her soul she knows it is.

The present slammed into me, knocking the breath out of me. My chest burned as I tried and failed to suck in much-needed gulps of air.

"Lana! Are you okay? You just glowed! Like, your skin!" Jensen screamed as she went to grab me.

"NO!" I blurted. I couldn't take another vison, not right then.

She froze without touching me. We both just looked at one another.

"Jensen, I have a lot to explain, but I can't right now. I swear I will, but for now I have to call my dad." I was out of breath, and every part of me felt raw and exposed.

Her face twisted up in disgust. "Lana," she intoned in that chiding way of hers.

"I know, but I can't explain until I talk to him."

She looked at me for another long moment before making her way to the door. I knew she was feeling dejected, but I had to talk to my dad. As soon as the door clicked shut behind her, I reached over to the floating table and fumbled for my phone.

I clicked it on and saw forty-six missed calls. All from my dad.

Without checking for any messages, I called him.

"Lana? Oh, thank the gods." I hadn't spoken to my father in five years; even still, his voice took me back to all the times he'd yelled at me for dropping a fork or one of the number of other things a child does. Or the times he'd come home drunk and angry. From the way he slurred his words, he was likely currently inebriated.

"Dad?" It was an all-encompassing question.

"She's dead. Your grandmother is dead."

Not that I needed him to tell me. I knew by the power I felt running through me that felt like pins and needles, as if my skin had fallen asleep and was waking up.

"I know. How?" I rasped.

My grandmother wasn't my direct grandmother. She was my great-great-great-great-grandmother. While normal women of her age would be long since gone, mine was the sacred oracle. I'd always known this was a possibility, as the power traveled down the matriarchal line, but I honestly never thought it would happen. From the time I was little before my mom died, she'd told me about my grandmother and how she'd been blessed with a gift from the gods, as she'd put it. We could trace our bloodline back to that of the Oracle of Delphi. Our bloodline was created long ago by the gods themselves, to offer a link between the people and the gods. This was a secret story in our family; one I knew but never fully believed. Well, by Hades's bouncing balls, I believed now, that's for damn sure.

"I, uh, don't know. I tried calling you. Where are you?" His third-degree line of questions rankled slightly.

"The hospital. I had a seizure in class." I sighed nonchalantly.

"You need to get out of there and get to, uh, where was that town she lived in?" He rambled, not caring one bit about the fact that I was in the damn hospital. I had to grit my teeth at him telling me fuck all. To say that we had a rocky relationship would be putting it lightly. The man had no idea about Havenwood Falls or on most days his own damn name.

My grandmother lived in a small town in Colorado. This was a special town, as it were, a place where supernaturals ran rampant and outsiders were discouraged. The whole town even had wards so no one could wander in without someone knowing about it or leave without forgetting it. I was sent there when I was seven to visit with my ya-ya and came home with a small tattoo so that I'd have the memory of how to get back if I needed to, though I would only regain those memories should my ya-ya ever die. Under normal circumstances, if someone in the town left, the tattoo would disappear along with their memories, but my grandmother petitioned the Court of the Sun and the Moon to have the Luna Coven weave a more permanent magic into my tattoo, one that would activate when she died. The Court rejected the petition at first, but she offered them something in return that seemed to change their minds, though I never knew what. Clearly my ya-ya's insistence that my mother force me to go made sense, despite how pissed my mom was when she found out her ulterior motive. The knowledge and memories of that time with my ya-ya were so clear now, I felt a little dizzy.

"Yeah, I know." I didn't know what else to say. My whole life was over. I'd always known it was possible the power might shift to me, but given my ya-ya had been the oracle for so long, I thought it wasn't likely. I thought I'd get to live a life that was all mine, one I picked. Glancing down at my tape-coated hand and legs covered by a scratchy thin sheet, I realized just how over my life really and truly was.

Then there was Jensen. I'd have to leave her behind. That thought alone caused my eyes to burn with hot tears. She'd been my oldest and best friend. I couldn't just leave her. But really, what choice did I have? It wasn't like I could bring her. She had a future, a life to live. My mind flashed the vision of her in that white dress. She had a wedding. Maybe once I settled down, I'd try to convince her to come up there.

"Lana, you there?" my dad wondered.

"Not really." It was the truth. I was somewhere, but my head was swimming and I couldn't cope.

"I want to see you." They were only five words, five words that snapped me back to reality.

"I haven't spoken to you in what? Five years? You know what you said to me?" It was a rhetorical question, one I didn't even give him a breath to think about. "You said, and I quote, 'Hey Lana, you owe me for those years I spent taking care of you.' You mean raising me? Or better yet, me raising myself. Remember that, Dad?"

"Lana—"

"No. You call me for money to spend on booze. Dad, I've been just fine without you, without mom, without anyone."

"I've changed—"

I hung up the phone and did the one thing I should have done nearly five years ago—I blocked him. I had no idea why it took so long to cut off such a toxic person, but it felt like a weight had been lifted off my chest.

I let my head fall back against the pillow, praying like hell I'd sink into sleep.

"Ms. Velis?" a male voice asked from what I assumed was the doorway.

"Unfortunately, yes," I muttered in a melancholy tone. *Just when I was trying to sleep or die, one of the two, ugh.*

The middle-aged man with thinning hair walked in to the room without meeting my eyes and started speaking. "Ms. Velis, we've done some tests, and everything we saw was normal."

He was glancing and flipping through some papers, still not meeting my eyes. I was a patient right in front of him, but he was treating me like a subject.

"Really? Normal? How odd, considering I'm half goblin and survive on nothing but Jell-O." He didn't even look up at me. I rolled my eyes so hard I thought I might actually need medical attention.

"I'd like to run a few more—"

"I'm going to stop you right there, Dr. Hubert." I had no idea what the hell his name was, but it didn't matter, as I was feeling slightly stabby. The use of his clearly incorrect name finally caused him to look at me for the first time.

"That's not my name," he interrupted, like a petulant child.

I held up a hand and shook my head.

"Well, it's not like you took the time to introduce yourself, did you? But that doesn't matter, because I'm out of here," I said coolly, as I glanced down at the IV on the side of my wrist. Pulling it free, I explained further, "There's nothing wrong with me. And yes, I know what AMA is and will sign whatever paperwork you'd like stating as much."

As I pulled the IV free, there was a small pinch and a tiny welling of blood. Pressing my thumb to the tiny hole in my skin, I looked at the wide-eyed doctor.

"Ma'am, I'm sorry, but I think you fail to grasp—"

"Oh, I grasp," I cut him off as I swung my legs over the side of the bed. It was then I realized I had no pants on. Glancing from my bare legs back to him, I decided I had zero fucks to give and, well, yolo.

Getting up, it wasn't until I bent over that I realized I hadn't been wearing panties that day. Well, either that or someone set the air conditioner to turbo. I whirled around to find the man looking at the spot my ass used to occupy. Wonderful. This day just kept getting better and better.

Gathering all my shit that had been stuffed into a too-small bag in my arms, I turned to face him.

"Trust me when I tell you, my health is the absolute least of your worries." *My sanity, though, is suspect*, I didn't add.

Brushing past him, I slipped on my flip-flops and cracked the door but paused at his frantic rambling.

"Ma'am, I, um could you please um, put pants on."

"I don't have time for your—" I paused when I realized that in that short span of time, I'd forgotten I didn't have pants on, again.

After pants and paperwork, I broke free from the hospital. I made Jensen leave earlier for her last final, so I had to figure my own way out. My exit was complicated by brushing past a homeless woman and seeing her future. I concealed my silvery white glowing self with my large book bag and ran out to my Uber as if my ass were on fire.

On the way back to the apartment I shared with Jensen, I called her to be sure she was at home. She was, and boy was she pissed I'd checked myself out of the hospital.

After I hung up with Jensen, I spent the rest of the drive trying to come up with a million and one explanations. But as I sat down right in front of her, none of them seemed to make sense or be good enough for my friend. They just seemed like a pack of lies she didn't deserve.

So there we sat in our living room that was filled with furniture we'd gotten from many weekends of thrift store shopping for a home we'd built together. I began feeling sick. This wasn't supposed to happen. This was supposed to be just like my mom: I'd get to live my own life. Even if she did die long before she should have, she at least had a life that was her own.

"You just going to sit there and ignore the white zebra in the room?" she puzzled as she glared at me.

"I think you mean white elephant. And isn't that a Christmas thing?" I quipped, hoping to prolong the inevitable.

Rolling her eyes, she huffed, "You know what I mean, so stop stalling."

"I'm not stalling." I was absolutely stalling. We both knew it.

"Listen here, you turd muffin, I don't know what's going on or why you checked yourself out of the hospital—"

I opened my mouth to tell her I hadn't, a lie. But she held up a hand, staving me off.

"Don't even try to tell me you didn't. Don't lie to me." She was beyond annoyed. She carried that tone she always had when she knew I was lying.

"Jensen, I—" The words caught in my throat. I didn't need to possess the power of the sacred oracle to see what was going to happen. I could see it play out in front of me.

Then something my ya-ya told me the only time I met her washed over me with the force of a rogue wave.

"You can't keep her forever, Lana." She sighed as she touched my hand. My ya-ya should have been old and covered with wrinkles that told the tale of a well-lived life, but the power of the oracle kept her young and ageless.

"Huh?" I questioned, looking back up at her. Her blue eyes that matched my own showed her many many years of life, yet there was a spark of knowing.

Cupping my face in her hands, she smiled down at me before she placed a soft kiss on my cheek. Her deep chocolate hair tickled my ear as she leaned in to whisper.

"You'll know what I mean when you're grown."

Over the years, I thought about that moment often. I even thought it might have been Cassie. But looking at this moment with Jensen, I knew it was now. I knew it was her.

She sat there and studied my face for a long moment. I wanted to tell her that I had to leave everything and everyone behind to become an oracle. Not that that would sound crazy or anything. Damn, how I wanted to tell her the truth. I almost did at least a hundred different times. I knew I couldn't. This wasn't the life I wanted.

"I don't want this." The words left my lips before I could stop them.

"Don't want what? Lana, you're scaring me." Her voice was shaking. I was scaring myself, if I was honest.

"To leave you." The words came out garbled and on a half sob. By the look on her face and the tears rolling down her cheeks, she understood everything.

"I—" she started, but her voice cut off in a squeak. "I don't understand."

"My ya-ya, she died. I have to—"

"Oh, that's all?" She looked relieved, then seemed to realize her words. "No, I mean I'm sorry she passed, but you look like you're leaving forever."

I just looked at her for a long moment.

Her eyes went wide, and she stood up abruptly, causing her cell phone to clatter to the wood floor.

"You are coming back, right?" I could nearly feel her accelerated heartbeat in her voice.

"No," I whispered. The word hung in the air between us like a crowbar prying us apart.

Turning her back to me, she walked to the front door and reached for the knob.

"Wait!" I nearly yelped.

She did.

"Please let me explain?" I begged to her back. She didn't turn to face me but didn't move either.

"My ya-ya has a home and family business that I have to go look after. It's not really what I wanted either. But I have to go."

Turning, she crossed her arms over her chest.

"Fine," she snapped. "I'll just come with you."

Smiling and cocking a hip out, I reminded her, "You have to graduate, and you already got a job at that uptight private school, where you'll teach the rich and obnoxious, remember?"

"Nope. I'm good. I'll quit," she snipped back.

"You can't! But how about you give me a year? Just one. That way it won't look bad on your résumé. Then if you still want to come, we'll figure it out."

Strained silence fell over us again, but this time there was a feeling to it that was warm and tender.

"Deal. But will you come and visit?" she asked, dropping her arms and opening them to me.

Walking into her embrace, I held her tight. While I hugged her, I was careful not to touch her skin. I couldn't really control, nor did I understand exactly, what was happening to me.

"I will if I can. But we'll figure something out. I promise," I assured her, even though I knew how unlikely that really was.

We both just stood there and held on to the last thread of our friendship as though it were a lifeline, and in many ways it was.

There was a loud hiss and meowing that rang out, followed by a bright streak of white fur.

"What are we going to do with Hades?" she wondered as we both looked at my insane cat.

Hades had been my oh-my-god-my-biological-clock-is-going-wacky-despite-being-in-my-early-twenties adoption. The stark white cat flopped on his back and started kicking his back legs against the lace bra—

"Hey! Asshole, that's my bra!" I hissed. He just looked at me, glared his *eat shit and die* look, and kept up the lacy assault.

"Yeah, you're so taking him with you." She laughed. "I'm not going to miss having to buy new bras every week," she added as she pulled away.

"Yeah, I guess Hades is coming with me." The thought of shoving his big-balled butt into a carrier had me mentally looking for the Band-Aids and ointment.

"I love you. That won't change. And I promise as soon as things calm down, I'll be sure I get your ass up for a visit," I assured her. It was then I realized I'd likely never see Cassie again. That thought normally would have devastated me, but now I really wasn't bothered by it. Leaving Jensen, though—that would be a hell of a lot harder.

She was my everything for so long, but I had to let her live her own life.

"I know. I love you, too."

Hades meowed so loud the downstairs neighbors banged on the floor.

"I won't miss that, though," she added. We both laughed like wild hyenas, and that caused the neighbors to pound again.

Then we both broke out into our best Michael Flatley imitations with shitty Irish dancing. Ah, got to love being petty.

CHAPTER 3

"*H*oly shit." My jaw dropped to the floor. I'd been to Havenwood Falls one time for all of a single day. So my memories of the small Colorado town were fuzzy to say the least. I certainly didn't remember my grandmother's house being this uh, well, clearly she was a hoarder. Either that or she sold all kinds of wooden, porcelain, glass, or you-name-it dolls. Creepy dolls, the stuff nightmares are made of.

Huffing, I set Hades's carrier on the floor and went to flip another light on. Pausing, I thought better of it. There was no way on earth I really wanted to see the billion and two eyes of the scary-ass doll things looking at me.

"Okay, Hades. We're home, er, home-ish."

He hissed. *Yeah, we're both just pleased as punch to be here.*

Opening his small cage, I prepared for his release, but he didn't budge. I peeked in to find him eyeing the small dolls that seemed to line every single space of the house.

"Same, buddy. Same." I sighed as I stood up. There was a stack of mail on the side table that caught my attention.

Flipping through the envelopes, I realized they were all addressed to me. *Just how long had the crazy lady known she was going to die?* Then

I realized there was a small journal with a post-it note stuck to the front that read, "Step one, read me."

Picking it up, I laughed. "I thought step one was to cut a hole in the box."

Well, according to Justin Timberlake anyway. *Guess it's not that kind of party. Pity.*

Hades growled in response.

"Man, I hate it when no one is around to hear my jokes. It's just a shame, honestly." I sighed again.

I grabbed the book, decided all the shit in my car could wait, and walked over to the flower-covered couch.

"Oh man, there's going to need to be a serious purge in our future, Hades," I commented as I sat down. Hades finally decided to leave his cage and jump up on my lap.

Stroking his short silky fur with one hand, I opened the book with the other. Ya-ya's handwriting wasn't familiar to me, but by the time I finished this instruction manual, I would never be able to forget it.

Lana,

I've known this day was coming since the moment you were born.

"Of course she did," I murmured as my eyes rolled.

Don't be snotty. It's not nice.

My eyes squinted at the paper. Had she just? Hades picked that moment to protest loudly about the fact that I'd stopped petting him.

I read on while stroking the testy cat.

I know you had plans—big ones. You planned to get your degree in graphic design and land a job at that advertising firm, the one that tends to hire only women. I'm sorry things didn't work out the way you'd hoped.

"Understatement of the century, Ya-ya."

But the one thing I'm truly sorry for is Jensen. I know she's been your rock for many years, especially after your mother died. So for that I truly am sorry. But I have a feeling that loss will only be temporary.

I had to bite my lip to keep from sobbing.

Lana, I know you might have a few questions, so I will do my best to answer them. First, as to how I died. After I'd been the oracle for so long, the gods saw fit to give me a choice for all my years of service. I could relinquish my duty so that a new one might arise. In doing so I would be granted an afterlife with the gods, to wander the afterlife and be reborn at a time of my choosing. Or I could remain the oracle, denying you your future.

"Denying me a future? Just what does that mean?"

I know you don't understand, but you will. Okay, moving on. Your power could manifest in a number of ways. Knowing you, my guess is you're a touch oracle. You can prophesy by touching someone. This is both good and bad. You won't be able to control the power. However, you don't have to touch people, so that's something, right?

Narrowing my eyes at the tightly packed cursive, I pursed my lips. Not touching people—great, there goes my nonexistent sex life.

There are some rules. First, if you see a future you may not do anything to affect that outcome. You must let the Fates cut their threads no matter what. This is the most important of our laws. You may not expound a vision unless that person, or persons, has been printed on the waitlist. Lana, understand the gods are great, but you are their link to the world. You are their gift to the humans. They will not hesitate to rain hell on earth should you break a sacred law.

Well, that sounded ominous.

You will find the list of petitioners in a spreadsheet on the computer in your room. I know, fancy, right?

I giggled in response. I wished suddenly I'd gotten to know my ya-ya more.

Okay, law two: you must be honest with each and every petitioner who comes to you. What they do with the information is up to them. Also, it's your duty to keep everything you see in utter confidence.

This was all a little too much information all at once. It was getting late, and I was beyond exhausted, but I read on. My grandmother went on to explain about the town and the deal she'd struck with the Court, which held dominion over the town. Basically, if they allowed her to live in the town and live within the protection offered, and also allow her petitioner a day pass with memories intact of the oracle's reading, there would be a permanent place for the Court on the list, should they ever need it.

I know all of this is new and even a little scary, but you won't be in this alone. When there is a new oracle, she is granted a protector, a guard—"

There was a pounding at the door that sent my heart to my throat and Hades's claws into my thighs.

"Ouch!" I hissed, hopping to my feet. The cat tumbled to the floor, hissed at me, and sauntered off to wherever the hell cats go.

The next knock nearly caused me to pee my damn pants. I didn't know anyone out here so it wasn't like I could have pissed anyone off. *Oh, dear gods, what if it's a serial killer? I've never seen one before but based on every documentary ever it could be. Oh, I guess he wouldn't knock before serial killing. Wait, do they knock at all?* For fuck's sake, my thoughts were rambling.

Creeping over to the door, I crouched low, then realized what a freaking moron I was being and stood up. Reaching for the doorknob, I thought better of it and grabbed a particularly heinous looking brass doll that was sitting on a small bookshelf. If nothing else, I'd scare whoever it was away with bad taste.

"Who's there?" I coaxed, realizing the damn door didn't have a peephole.

"Pizza man," a deep, rolling voice crooned.

Pizza? I didn't order a pizza. I mean, if it's a mistake, I could just take the pizza. I do love pizza. Wait, no, that's dumb. By Hades's bouncing balls, I was being ridiculous.

"I didn't order a pizza," I called back.

Then the damn guy laughed. He fucking laughed at me! He had some nerve.

Tossing the door open, I shoved the creepy doll in his face and waggled it menacingly. Well, as menacingly as one could look whilst waving a bronze doll.

"Hey! I don't appreciate being made fun of. It's been a long day and —" My words were cut off when I finally got a look at the man behind the deep voice. He had long—by what I'd call guy standards—brown hair that hung in his eyes. From what I could see, he had light brown eyes that were a shade lighter than his hair. But it wasn't his eyes that caused me to pause. It was his smile. He had this wide grin that was a mix of sex and the Cheshire cat. He stood a full foot—if not more—taller than me, so I had to adjust my weapon's aim, not that'd I'd really call it a weapon.

My frantic waggling seemed to only amuse him. Dropping the horrific doll to my side, I cocked out my foot and put my other hand on my hip.

"You know, I spent a whole summer at karate camp when I was ten. And I'll have you know, I could kick your"—I let my eyes roam over him to gauge his size. While he was lean to the eye, he held himself like a man who knew how to use his body in all kinds of ways —"your tall ass from here to Sunday. So, unless you have a really, and I do mean *really* good reason for being here, I suggest you mosey on back to the underside of the bridge you call home."

Other than his eyebrows twitching up about a half a millimeter and his lips tilting up slightly, he looked utterly unfazed.

"I think I have a pretty good reason. I'll let you be the judge, though." His voice oozed cockiness. *Oh, this is why I never dated men. Well, never say never, but that's certainly why I didn't date men like this douche goblin.*

Reaching a hand out to me, he gave me a wide smile before adding, "Hi, I'm Damen Costos, the new guardian to the sacred oracle."

We both just stood there for a moment too long, him with his hand out and me like a moron, just looking at it. *There's no way I can shake his hand. He's going to think I'm a douche. Oh well.*

Lifting his hand, he ran the large fingers through his long dark locks instead.

"Well, you are the new oracle, aren't you?" he queried, now looking a little confused. He did, however, take a very long look at me.

"Yeah, I am. Sorry, come in. It's just been a long day, and I'm a little frazzled." Understatement of the century. There had been a lot of those lately. I pivoted so that he could enter. His eyes went from me to the area behind me, then back to me.

"Not really a decorating choice I'd make, but to each their own. How about you show me to my room?" he mumbled, just before walking in.

There are these moments in life when everything slows down, and you're met with perfect clarity. This wasn't that moment; in fact, this was just the opposite. Everything hit me all at once and spiraled out of control. The reality was I'd erected an emotional dam, and all the shit had piled up.

"Are you fucking kidding me?" Dam broken.

I held up a hand, stopping him from speaking.

"You know what? I don't even care if you're kidding me or not. But I'm done. I'm so freaking done. I don't want to be here. I had everything ripped from me. I was moments away from graduating. I had to leave my best friend behind. And I caught my girlfriend cheating on me about a week ago. You just walk into my house, informed me you're my new roommate, and you're worried about whether or not I fluffed your pillows? Do you even know my name? You know what, go take a flying fuck!" I was heaving and huffing, I was so pissed.

"Wait," he called as I turned my back on him. Damn him if he thought I'd give up one single tear on his account. I did stop, though.

"You're a lesbian?"

I threw my hands in the air, hoping the gods would just go on and strike me down to put me out of my misery.

Facing him, I nearly exploded, "Really? Out of everything I just said, the fact that I was in a relationship with a girl is what you latched on to? The fact I date who I like—that's what you have an issue with? How about, 'Hi, my name is douche canoe,'" I mimicked in a mock male tone.

His eyes went wide for a split second before they returned to the indifferent expression he'd been sporting moments before. I, however, surely looked like the wild and crazy oracle I was. I was breathing hard, seriously pissed off.

Shaking his head, he replied, "No, it's not that. I'm from a small town, and no one is ever open like that. I guess it caught me off guard."

A thick silence fell over the small space, making it feel yet smaller. My anger began to ebb, and I realized just how out of line my outburst had been. This really wasn't the introduction I wanted.

"Listen, how about we sit down and start over? I'm coming across like a total asshole," he finally said, breaking the silence.

"Yeah, you are, but I'm not much better, so I agree. Let's start over."

An expression flashed across his face, but it happened so fast, I wasn't sure I saw anything at all.

"Hi, I'm Damen. And if it makes you feel better, I too had to leave a life behind," he greeted once more.

We sat down on the plastic-covered couch. Before I had time to reply, Hades rounded the corner and hopped up on the coffee table, likely to inspect the newcomer. The cat leaned forward to sniff the air near Damen. The tall man reached out to allow Hades to smell him. Hades, being the turd he was, drew in a little air, then hissed.

Yanking his hand back, Damen growled, "What's wrong with your cat?"

"Everything. Who knows, really? Hades isn't really a fan of people . . ." My words trailed off as the damn cat hopped off the table and onto Damen's lap, then curled up into a ball and proceeded to purr. The devil of a cat actually, honest to god, purred.

My mouth gaped open in both shock and betrayal. *Et tu, Hades?*

"Guess your pussy likes me after all."

I groaned at his play on words. This was going to be a really long night, er, eternity.

"Lana," I blurted out like a total moron.

"The cat's name?" he asked, as one eyebrow bolted upward and his brow furrowed in confusion.

"No, mine. I realized I never told you. He's Hades."

"Well, nice to meet you both," he stated, holding out a hand for me to shake. I just stared at it.

"Sorry, not to be rude, but I can't touch you. Apparently, that's how this lovely gift of mine has manifested." The girl who can't be touched. Sounds like an Amish romance title—groan.

Smiling, he assured me, "You can't see my future. So don't worry about that."

"Oh" was all I could say.

"Let me explain. I've been training for my role as guardian my whole life. Just as your power goes down the line of females in your family, the role of the protector of the oracle travels down the line of males in mine. We are granted the strength of Hercules. While we stop aging, like you, we aren't immortal. I was created to protect you— protect the gift the gods have given to the mortals. My life is now tied to yours."

He knew so much more about this life than I did. How was this possible? Well, if I was being honest, the answer was my mother. After the one visit I had, coming back with a tattoo, my mother wanted nothing to do with what she'd called the tall tale of our family, though I'd always known it was true. It wasn't like I had much time with her. Shortly after that, she left me with my drunk dad, then died a few years after that.

"You didn't know any of this, did you?" Concern was threaded in his question.

"Not really. I came up here one summer for one visit. My ya-ya told me about the power she had. She said someday I might get it. Then she petitioned the Court to give me a tattoo. They put it here." I lifted my hair up, exposing the back of my neck. "Once my mom found out about my new ink, that was it. My mom refused to hear anything about Havenwood Falls, our family power, or anything. I never heard anything more from my grandmother until recently, but I guess I thought it was disrespectful to my mom's memory, so I ignored her." I rubbed the bridge of my nose, hoping that the headache forming would ebb. Looking back on my actions, I realized how utterly stupid and childish I'd been. Hindsight really was twenty-twenty.

"So what do you know?" He lazily stroked Hades's velveteen ears.

"Honestly, I knew I could possibly get the power. And I knew of Havenwood Falls; well, I did after I received my power anyway. Oh and it wasn't like, boom here's your power and cookie, nope, not for me. I had a full-on seizure in class, then I saw the future of my best friend when I touched her. Other than that, I have no idea what I'm doing."

Running a big hand through his long hair, he sighed.

"You might have wanted this. But I didn't."

His brown eyes went wide, then narrowed slightly at my words. "I never said I wanted this. I wanted to make music. I wanted to perform. But I have a responsibility to my family, to the gods, to humans, and to you. Hell, you at least had a tattoo, making it somewhat easy to get here. I had a hand-drawn map my grandfather left me. I'd never even met the man before. Despite all of that, I very much take all of this seriously."

"And I don't?" I snapped. It came out way harsher than I'd meant, but damn, was he saying I didn't care? I was here, wasn't I?

"That's not what I'm saying," he hurried, his expression hardening.

"Listen I don't think anything you or I say at this point is going to help. How about we just go get some sleep? I think there's an inn somewhere in town." I let the statement fall off at his raised eyebrow.

"The guardian lives with the oracle. I have to be near you always," he explained, raising an eyebrow.

"You are *not* sleeping with me!" I very nearly screamed. My tone must have been surprising, as Hades jolted off of his lap, but by how Damen's face was contorted, he'd left him a parting gift with all of his claws before vacating.

"You say that now, princess." He winked as he stood up and brushed the fur off his lap. His eyes tracked over to the cat, who sauntered off.

"Holy big balls, Batman!" he exclaimed.

"Yeah, it's a whole thing. They're fake. It's a really long story." I groaned.

I had a new weird power with all kinds of rules. I had to leave everything I knew behind. I lived in a town where I knew absolutely no one. I had a new house and a massive list of people to see. And to top that shit-coated cone? I had a new roommate.

I glanced at his ass as he walked through the room to explore what I guessed was his new home. With a behind like that, it couldn't all be bad, could it?

"Take a picture. It will last longer," he hollered.

Yeah, I guess it could be that bad. Ugh.

CHAPTER 4

"Oh, for the gods' damn sake, would you hurry the hell up?" I screamed at the closed door. Not that I was really angry at the door itself, rather the man behind it. He'd been in there since the beginning of time, so needless to say, I was over it.

"What kind of house only has one bathroom?" he grumbled in an almost inaudible tone.

"I didn't exactly pick the layout, if you must know. However, I'm about to pee myself so—" My words trailed off as the oak door swung open. In a plume of steam stood Damen with only a towel that hung low on his hips. I couldn't have stopped my eyes from trailing down his well-defined chest to his oh by Hades's bouncing balls—

"Sorry. As I'm sure you can see, perfection takes time." His voice dripped cockiness. It would have been seriously impressive had it not been so infuriating.

I groaned so hard I might have actually seen stars from the lack of oxygen.

"Yeah, well, in that case you might want to hop your happy ass right back in there." With each word I spoke, his smile grew. Clearly my joking amused him.

"I like you." He chuckled before walking away.

Men are so confusing; I might have to stick to women.

A shower never felt so damn good. The heated water almost made me forget that I had an unwanted roommate, an unwanted power, and an unwanted life.

"Ugh, now I'm just being whiny," I said to absolutely no one, but nevertheless it was true.

Hades meowed a long drawn-out howl as if in reply. Clearly, he agreed even though he wasn't asked. But he was kinda right.

Sticking my head out of the shower, I spotted the white cat splayed out in, of all places, the sink. Lucky for him, the water wasn't on.

"Okay, Hades, I swear, from here on out I won't do the woe is me. And I'll try to have a more positive outlook on this whole situation. And I need to apologize to Damen. He hasn't deserved my hostility one damn bit. Happy now?" I assured the cat while blinking the water from my vision.

He picked that moment to tuck his head down and hike his back leg up as he proceeded to lick his massive manhood, er, cathood. I took that as a yes and finished my shower.

When I came out of my room, I saw Damen sitting on the couch, strumming an acoustic guitar.

I couldn't quite tell what he was playing, so I sat down and listened to him.

The melody was haunting and had such an old-world feel that it caused my whole body to break out into goose bumps. As the speed of his fingers picked up, the intensity of the song built to a fever pitch. My heart mimicked the frantic beat. I could feel myself leaning toward him for something more, anything more. Fuck, just more.

Then everything just stopped. His fingers froze, hovering just above the cords. The only thing I could hear in the small space was my own heartbeat. His gaze was locked on mine, and for a moment, I felt solid and grounded. I didn't feel like I'd just float away, for once.

Hades came skittering into the room. He paused, looking at the two of us, hissed, and ran back out.

"That cat has some serious issues."

"Are you a bard?" The question just kind of fell out. I thought it was possible, considering how enraptured he had me.

"No, but I'm glad you liked it, because I wrote it."

Silence fell over the small space, making it seem even smaller.

"Listen, I'm sorry for my attitude. I won't try to justify it. I'm dealing with things the best way I know how and took it out on you. Just give me a little time to adjust. Everything has happened so fast." He deserved an apology. He didn't deserve the crap I'd given him over the past day.

Laying down his guitar, he moved so that he was crouched in front of me. I had no idea why, but butterflies erupted in my stomach. *Stupid insects.*

He offered his hand to me, but I didn't move. I couldn't. I knew he'd told me that I couldn't see his future because it was tied to mine, but I wasn't sure. There were so many rules that I still knew nothing about.

"Trust me. You don't have to, but I want you to. Our lives are intertwined, but you still have a choice. And I want your choice to be to trust me." I knew he hadn't meant to, but his words gutted me. They were nearly the same words that Cassie had fed me so long ago. I couldn't help my body's reaction—I flinched.

His hand and head dropped at nearly the same time.

"Someone said those same words to you, didn't they?" He didn't meet my eyes.

"How?" was all I could croak out.

"I don't have to be an oracle to see pain." Then his eyes met mine. Offering me his hand again, he added, "Just give me a chance to earn your trust."

I couldn't allow the sins of another to cloud how I saw him, and that's what I was doing.

Taking his hand, I nodded. It was only when I felt his warm skin against mine that I realized that this had been the first person, since Jensen, I'd touched. It made me sad to think how careful I'd have to be. Would I be able to touch anyone again?

He didn't pull his hand from mine. He only squeezed it reassuringly.

While I couldn't see his future directly, icy fear washed over me, causing me to pull my hand from his.

"We need to get going." I half coughed.

"Where to?" he asked, standing up.

"We have a meeting with the Court of the Sun and the Moon. We have to go over the compact we have with them. Just to be sure we're allowed to operate the same way my ya-ya did." Hell, for once, I sounded like I knew what the crap I was talking about. Hey, fake it till you make it, right?

The town really was adorable, from what little I was able to see of it. It'd been so long since I'd been here, and I mostly remembered my mom and Ya-ya fighting, so I never really took note of the town. The place had a quaintness about it, though my skin pricked with the amount of supernatural energy pulsing through it.

I moved around a lot as a kid, never really staying in one place for too long, so I knew when a town had a heartbeat. This one did. The people seemed to move around as if they were blood flowing in veins, giving the place life. I couldn't help but smile. *No, it hadn't really been in my plan to give up my hard-fought college degree at the very last second, abandon my best and only friend, and—* Nope, I wasn't going down this trail of thought. I was going to make the best of this and make the active choice to be happy.

"Earth to Lana." Damen's voice cut through my thoughts like the annoying squeal of a cat in heat.

"Sorry, what?" I was perplexed, looking from his eyes to the object he held out to me.

"Here, before we do a whole lot, I want you to put these on," he instructed me, sternly waggling the gloves at me.

Raising an eyebrow, I puzzled, "Uh, why? It isn't even that cold out. It's August, for crap's sake." If I put those babies on, I'd end up with major clam hands.

"Because when we meet with the Court, I'd like you to not be rude and be able to shake their hands. Plus, we don't know the extent of your abilities. What if you touch a door handle after someone else. Could you get a reading that way? Do you know?"

I paused at his words. The truth was, I had no idea. This was all so new to me. I had my ya-ya's journal, but when the power moves from one oracle to the next, it becomes unique to her. I looked at him. I half expected him to have a smug, knowing smile ready to gloat that he was right, but what I saw in him caused me to stop. It was genuine caring I saw staring back at me. His job was to protect me. He was under no obligation to like or even care about me, but he did.

"You're right." I sighed.

I grabbed the slender leather gloves and slipped them on.

"Come on, short stuff, I saw a bakery not far from here. We'll get some food and OJ." Grabbing my hand, he pulled me along. Under normal circumstances, I would have objected, but I found my fingers curling around his without much thought. *How peculiar.*

"Daily Knead. That's such a cute name."

"Let's hope they have something to feed the bear, because I'm hungry!" Damen half laughed as he pushed the door open.

A delightful tinkling sounded as the door swung open. The bright white of the tile made the small space seem bigger than I knew it was.

"Welcome to the Knead!" a cheerful voice called out. As much as I wanted to return the gesture of greeting, the pictures that lined the walls caught my eye. There were several black-and-white images of the town that seemed to span who knew how many years. Finally, after what was far too long, I glanced to the left side of the shop. There behind the counter stood a dark-haired girl who couldn't have been more than about eighteen, whose name tag read *Meghan.*

"Hi! Thank you. Sorry, I got so distracted by the pictures. They're beautiful," I explained, looking over to the opposing wall. There, where I'd just come from, stood Damen, who also seemed captivated by the photos.

"Aren't they? I swear every time I come in here, I see something I haven't seen before." She giggled with a wide smile.

We both grinned. She had a kind of sweet innocence about her that led me to believe she had to be fully human. Not that that was a bad thing.

"What would you like today?" she asked, looking up at the menu posted behind her.

My eyes went wide at all the options.

"Oh my gosh. Wow, you guys have a ton!"

"Yeah, Michelle is practically a witch in the kitchen." She laughed at her own joke. There was just something so endearing about her.

"How about a cinnamon roll? And—"

"Make that two, and two cups of orange juice. Please and thank you!" Damen chimed in.

"Got it," she replied brightly.

Taking the cash Damen handed her, she popped the register open, then turned to walk to the back of the store.

"Shall we sit?" I asked, walking over to a small round table.

A few moments later, Meghan walked over and set down our food and drinks. "I hope you enjoy it!"

"Thank you," Damen replied.

Without another word, we both dove in. It was the perfect mix of sweet meets cream meets spice. It was far and away the best cinnamon roll I'd ever had.

A soft chuckling pulled me out of my cinnamon-induced stupor. Opening my eyes, that at some point I'd shut, I saw Damen's grin.

"What?" I questioned, frowning.

"Oh, nothing. Just figured out the way to your heart is cinnamon rolls."

Scoffing, I replied indignantly, "Nuh-uh." I know—not my wittiest reply, but hey, I was mad he was right. But what he didn't know was any sweet would do.

Then, out of nowhere, he reached out and swept a thumb across my bottom lip. My heart sped up for some crazy reason.

Raising his finger up, he smirked. "Icing." He then dipped his digit in his mouth to clean it off. A fucking meteor could have hit the whole damn town and yet my attention would still have been glued to him.

"I hope you guys are enjoying your food." The woman's voice was like a bucket of ice water, one I clearly needed.

Sucking in a gulp of air, I looked over at the new woman. She had long wavy dark hair and kind brown eyes. If I had to say, I would have pegged her for somewhere north of thirty-seven or so.

"Oh my gosh, I think these are the best cinnamon rolls I've ever had. I don't know who made them, but they need a raise." My mouth watered at the idea of ordering seconds.

The woman let out a loud bark of laughter. After a moment, she said, "Well, I'll be sure to take that under advisement, considering it was me."

"Oh!" It was then I realized her name tag read *Michelle*. The either literal or metaphorical witch in the kitchen.

"Are you guys new to town?" She smoothed down a flour-coated apron.

"Yes, ma'am. Just got here yesterday," Damen mumbled around a gooey bite of sugary confection.

Shaking my head, I said, "Please excuse his manners. He was raised in a barn by wild hogs."

"True story!" he hollered, while raising a hand with a clenched fist. The action sent something flying from his lips to the table. By Hades's bouncing balls, he was an absolute mess.

Michelle, however, just giggled.

"Well, welcome. I'm Michelle Price, and you already met Meghan." She smiled, sticking out a hand in greeting.

I returned the gesture. "It's nice to meet you. I'm Lana, and this reprobate is Damen. Like he said, we just got here last night. We live in a cabin on the outskirts of town. My ya-ya died, and we came to uh, take over her business," I tried to explain, but my words came out in a jumbled mess. It was hard to tell if she was human or something else. While I might have been human, I was god-touched. I was a gift, as were my abilities.

She gave me a knowing smile, and I swear I saw her wink.

"Well, let me know if you need anything. Oh, I almost forgot. I think there will be a ghost tour tonight. It might be a great way to learn more about our lovely town."

"Oh, that would be fun!" I sang in a bright voice. I knew in that moment this might be a place I could fall in love with.

"Thanks!" Damen garbled, sending a half-chewed chunk of cinnamon roll flying across the table to land smack dab on Michelle's apron. Oh, good gods, please no.

Nearly choking, Damen coughed, cleared the possible obstruction, and rasped, "Sorry, it's just so good."

She smiled at him, then me as I mouthed, "I'm sorry." She just chuckled as she walked away.

"Damen, if first impressions were left up to you, I think we'd be sincerely screwed."

"Who's to say we aren't?" he moaned suggestively, while waggling his eyebrows. The poor tufts of hair looked like scared caterpillars quivering on his forehead. I groaned as if in pain. And this was what I had to look forward to for eternity. Fucking lovely.

CHAPTER 5

"*D*ude, relax, would you? You're making me nervous," Damen whispered, so close to my ear I felt the warm puffs of air from his words against my skin, sending a shiver up my spine.

"You're not helping!" I snapped. I couldn't help it. I was so stressed about this damn meeting. If they didn't agree to the compact, we'd have to move. I mean, what if I screwed the whole thing up? Where would we go? I had a job to do and a billion-year-long, ever-growing petitioner list.

"I can practically hear your thoughts," he added annoyingly.

Glaring at him, I opened my mouth to reply, but the double doors swung open. I swallowed hard, hoping that would ease the lump that had formed in my throat. No such luck.

Damen grabbed my arm as we were getting up and pulled me to him.

"I feel what you feel. That's our connection as oracle and guardian. I'm here to protect you. I won't let them, or anyone, hurt you. Trust me." His words acted like a balm to my overreacting anxiety. His eyes studied me, and in that moment, his words hit me full force. He was so many things, but he'd always be here to protect me.

I nodded and relaxed slightly.

"There's my girl." He sighed with a smirk, which didn't cause a bazillion and six butterflies to erupt in my stomach or anything.

"Ms. Valis?" a small feminine voice rang out.

"That's me!" I exclaimed, like a total moron.

"This way, but your, uh, friend will have to stay."

I felt Damen stiffen at her statement.

"I'm sorry. I'm afraid that's simply not possible. This is Damen. He's my guardian. If I go, he goes. If he stays, I stay," I stated with absolute authority. Even my own tone shocked me, but this was my place in life now. I had to abide by the rules set on the oracle.

"Fine," the woman sneered, before moving out of the way and gesturing toward the open room.

This was it, now or never. Damen placed his hand at the small of my back and lightly pushed me. We both walked in.

Eleven members of the court sat down behind a long table. Eleven separate pairs of eyes sat staring back at me disapprovingly. Well, maybe not all of them, but some of them did for sure.

"Uh, hi?" It came out a question. Fuck, I was such an idiot. *Uh, hi? Ugh.*

A woman who looked to be my age with dark brown hair and an odd gray-green stare smiled softly at my words. My grandmother had listed the names of the Court members, but there weren't any descriptions, so I really had no idea who anyone was.

"You're the new Oracle of Delphi?" a dark-haired man scoffed. This time I was pretty sure there was disapproval in his tone. There was something in his blue eyes. Maybe it was the way he looked at me or maybe it was my own insecurities, but I suddenly felt like an ant under a magnifying glass, and this prick was the kid holding it.

"Uh, either that or I need to be heavily medicated." *Ugh!* My hand flew to cover my mouth. Shit was just coming out without my permission.

"Oh, for crap's sake, Roman! Could we just not scare her?" the smiling woman from before snapped.

"How about we just introduce ourselves and you can do the same. Let's start there," a slender woman sporting some seriously big hair groaned. In turn, they all gave their names. The smiling girl was Michaela Petran. She looked to be my same age. I couldn't help but smile at her when it was her turn to talk. She was engaging and had a strong air about her, someone I wanted to get to know.

Not everyone on the Court exuded her gripping personality. The gruff man was Roman Bishop. Frankly, he scared the shit out of me. However, I thought that's just who he was, very intense. Damen didn't seem to have a reaction at all, except to one man.

When Lawrence Mills addressed me, I could feel aggression and disgust waving off of the man. Damen's hand gripped mine tightly, and he even shifted slightly as if to ready himself. It was an action I was sure wasn't missed by the rest of the Court.

After the Court finished the introductions, it was my turn.

"I'm Lana Velis. I am the oracle, gift of the gods to the mortals. I'm new to all of this, as my mother made the choice to keep me away for so long. My ya-ya and her guardian passed away recently, and the power of the oracle has passed to me. While I'm long-lived, I am granted a new guardian. This is Damen Costas. We're here to renegotiate the terms of the compact that was signed by my grandmother and this Court many years ago." My voice may have been steady and confident, but my heart was beating like the hooves of a wild horse.

There was an uncomfortable pause before Roman spoke up.

"So just because your grandmother had a contract with us, we're supposed to grant you one?" While he came off kinda like an asshole, I thought his question had merit.

"In the end, that's up to you. What I'm asking for is a place to live. My grandmother left me her home, on the outskirts of town. I would like to reside there, honor the petitioners who on my official list, and do my job," I explained, though I knew there was more to it.

"And what exactly would our town get from allowing something like this? Letting outsiders flood our borders with their memories intact sounds like it would be a crack in the foundation our town is built on," Ric Kasun asked. While his words were stern, his eyes glittered with kindness.

"The Court will have me. As with my grandmother, the Court will have a permanent place on my petitioner list, and should the need arise, I will be at your disposal. The way it works is I have a list. This list is incredibly, exceedingly, annoyingly, and infuriatingly long. The petitioners come in, I will do my thing, they will be able to stay in the town, bringing in money and such, then when they leave, they will lose their memory of the town, but not the reading they were given. I have laws I am bound to, so if someone isn't on my list and I see a future, I can't help them. If I see something damning, such as a threat to the town, my hands are bound. If the Court does not agree to these terms, there will be little I can do." Silence fell again as each member thought about my words. I could tell it wasn't so much that they didn't want me here, but that they had a big responsibility of protecting this place, the way of life, and the people in it. In an odd way, that thought alone helped me both relax and gave me the urge to be part of such a thing, such a community.

"Was that a threat?" Roman intoned calmly. Though his words were even, his glare was pointed, and his lips were pursed into a flat white line.

"Not at all. It was an explanation of power," I clarified.

Damen shifted to my right slightly, the same direction Roman sat. Roman's eyes, ever watchful, tracked the slight change, and he smirked.

"How do we even know she's got any kind of ability at all?" Roman added the question in a bored tone.

"He makes a good point. She was a human until days ago? What's to say anything has changed?" Lilith Blackstone added.

"Why not let her show you?" Damen snapped. I whipped my head to meet his gaze. I gave him a look that conveyed, *What the fuck are you thinking?* But he clearly didn't get it. He had no idea I'd only ever done this twice, and both were totally an accident.

"Oh! Yes!" Madame Tahini clapped her hands excitedly. Her motions sent her long, nearly black hair sliding in front of her face. She blew out a long breath, causing the strands to fly outward. "How about Mr. Loud Mouth? Mr. Roman could use an omen!" She was clearly pleased with herself.

"Well, I can't very well read anyone unless they agree, and . . ."

My words fell away as I saw Roman tent his fingers under his chin and a wicked smirk slowly spread on his face.

"I'm not a coward. Come, Lana, read me. Let's see if you can tell me something no one else knows." His words dripped with challenge.

Fuck my life. I stood there for a solid thirty seconds, unable to move. What if all I saw was that he was going to have a peanut butter and jelly sandwich for dinner? Or that he was going to break my face? Oh, by Hades's bouncing balls, I had to find a damn backbone and get the hell over this.

Finding that backbone I'd been missing, I walked over and removed my glove.

"I just need your hand," I informed him, unable to hide the shaking in my voice.

With utterly no emotion, he stuck his hand out for me.

Taking in a deep breath, I reached out and laid my hand on top of his.

A crash of crystal and china rang out as they fell to the floor, flooding the expensive-looking Persian rug with wine. He didn't seem to even notice the mess he'd made. His vibrant blue eyes were focused in such a way that went beyond obsession; he was like a shark stalking his prey. The woman sat on the edge of the table, her breathing shallow. There wasn't fear in her eyes, not the way they fell into a golden color then back again.

"Lie back," he ordered, his tone rough.

She paused at his words, and her breathing hitched.

Reaching back, he grabbed a fistful of her hair, angled her face to his, and snarled, "Lie. Back."

She allowed him to guide her back until she was splayed out for him like a goddamn meal. Releasing his grip on her hair, he took a slight step back to observe his prey. To feast with his eyes the meal he would devour. He could feel his need for her, and it only seemed to anger him.

"Part your legs." This time she didn't hesitate. She knew that tone. She knew that intent. Slowly she spread her thighs until her lace-clad sex was

bare to him. She had to stop her shiver. He'd only see that as weakness, and fuck if she'd ever show him anything other than strength.

He slid fingers up her silken thighs and she had to stifle a moan. He let his too-warm fingers dip down past the hem of her panties and yet lower. A moment later he pulled the lace down and stuffed his prize into his pocket. He could wait no longer. He needed to taste her. Without breaking away from her eyes, he slid his finger into his mouth.

He needed more. He'd have everything, all of her. He slid his hand back to her core. Parting her slightly, he found her clit and rubbed slow circles. Her eyes rolled back and her head fell lightly back to the hard wood table. It was then she felt his warm breath on her core. His mouth covered her as he began a slow feast of her. She didn't stifle her moan. There was no fucking way she could have.

I sucked in a deep breath of air as the erotic scene ended abruptly. I yanked my hand from his without much thought, just praying I wouldn't be pulled back in. I had to blink rapidly to coax my vision back. I could feel more than see everyone's gaze on me. I glanced down at my exposed hand to see its bright white glow begin to fade back to my normal tanned color. As the white glow receded, my face flooded with heat from such an erotic scene. I could feel everything he felt, everything she felt. It left me panting and embarrassed to have seen such a thing in front of so many people.

"Well," Roman's lips twitched. "Other than lighting up like a light bulb, what did the great Oracle of Delphi see?" His question was laced with a mix of amusement and disbelief.

"Uh . . ." I started, but stopped myself. Was this information something he really wanted spread far and wide? I could feel heat rush to my face. I had no freaking idea what to do. I glanced to Damen, who just stared at me. He was no help.

Taking a deep breath, I mumbled sheepishly, "Uh um, I think I'd like to tell you in private? This particular vision was, um, rather personal." I stammered around the words.

His eyes raised ever so slightly, something I would read as shock for this hard man. However, in others possibly, I would have questioned that I'd seen anything at all.

Roman nodded and motioned for me to walk over to him.

"Did Roman's omen turn him shy? Oh my!" Tahini giggled.

Roman shot her a death stare that it seemed she couldn't care less about.

Leaning down, I retold him everything I saw. While he didn't seem to have any reaction verbally, his hands tightened into fists.

Once I was done, I began my retreat, but Roman's hand flew out like lightning to snake around my wrist. Thankfully, he took care to keep his hand on the edge of my lightweight sweater. My heart rate went sky high as I heard Damen shuffle up. I reached out a hand to stop him. Looking over my shoulder, I caught his rage-filled gaze.

"I'm fine," I mouthed. While I knew it likely wouldn't matter, he did pause. Was his body getting bigger? I blinked, but returned my attention to Roman.

"Tell no one," he hissed, so low I thought it doubtful anyone else heard.

"It's my duty as sacred Oracle. All things are held in confidence," I assured him in a smooth confident tone that told nothing about the quivering mass of Jell-O I was feeling inside.

Clearly satisfied, he let me go, but not before glancing—and smirking—at Damen. It was the kind of expression that was meant to taunt him.

"Stop antagonizing him," I snapped at Roman. The words flew out of my mouth before I had a moment to stop them.

Michaela erupted in laughter. "Oh man, I like her. She's totally got my vote!"

"Please step out and allow us to debate and then we'll call you back in," Mathilde Augustine instructed politely.

As soon as the door closed, Damen snatched my hand and inspected it.

"I swear to the gods, if he hurt you . . ." he mumbled.

"I'm fine," I assured him. My words, however, didn't seem to stop him from fussing over me like a mother hen. It was both odd and a little exhilarating to have someone fuss over me. I was sure I'd never had anyone do that. Well, other than Jensen. My mother had left so early on, and my dad was always useless.

"Well, you look fine. But I'm here to tell you if he lays another hand on you . . ." He let the threat hang thick in the air.

"Did you, uh, get bigger back there?" I pulled my hand from his.

Running a hand through his hair, he nodded.

"Yeah, that happens when I see something as a threat to you. Well, I mean I knew it would, but that's the first time." It was then I realized this was all new to him, too. Just as unsure as I was, he was likely the same.

Cupping his face, I pulled his gaze to mine.

"You don't have to be okay with this. There isn't a rule or law that says you have to be. You know that, don't you?"

I couldn't explain it, but I could feel an overwhelming sense of peace fill me even at my own words. We always hear people ask are you okay; I'd always felt like I had to say yes and believe it.

His brown eyes searched mine for a long moment. For the first time, I saw the same fears and uncertainty in my own gaze reflected back at me.

"You can come back in." A voice wove its way into the spell that I'd unknowingly created. Neither of us moved right away.

After a long moment, I dropped my hands and backed away. Just as soon as I let go, I felt his hand tug on mine as he laced our fingers together.

"Come on, oracle."

Where he led, I found myself following, and oddly I was okay with it.

CHAPTER 6

The Court voted ten to one in my favor, though I didn't think Roman Bishop had been the one against.

With that meeting behind me, I was able to relax slightly. I had a place to live and a job to do, but for now I could just have a little fun and go on a ghost tour. Well, after a certain Damen got his fancy new tattoo. I didn't need one, as I'd already had mine at such a young age.

"Do you have any tattoos?" I inquired of Damen as we neared the exit of the Court chamber, stopping at the back of the room.

"No, you? I mean other than the one." His voice had this deep tone that reminded me of the distant rumbling of thunder rolling as a storm grew closer.

"Yeah, I have one other," I replied absentmindedly.

Reaching for the doorknob, he paused and quirked up an eyebrow in question.

Smiling, I reached for the door and opened it myself. Just before walking through I added in a flirty tone, "I guess you'll just have to find out what and where it is."

I had no idea what had possessed me. I couldn't help it.

He smirked and quipped, "Game on then, oracle."

Walking through the doorway, I saw a girl sitting at a small desk. As soon as we walked in, she smiled at us brightly. She had the kind of smile that made me want to smile back at her. Her light brown hair was in a mess of a bun atop her head, but there was a red bandana tied lovingly around her head in that way I'd seen a lot of pinup girls had done way back when. As if in direct contrast, her nose ring, black-rimmed glasses, and tattoo-covered arms seemed to stand out more.

"Hey there! You my first victim? Oh, I mean customer?" She laughed at her own joke, and I joined her.

Running his big hand through his shaggy hair, Damen coughed nervously. I narrowed my eyes at him. Was he afraid? Maybe he didn't like needles? I opened my mouth to jab at him, but then thought better of it. This man wanted to always put out a strong front.

"Yeah, I guess that'd be me." He half coughed.

"Well, I'm Addie, and I was the one over in the corner scribbling notes earlier. It's nice to meet you two, you know, not in a meeting." She smiled at Damen.

"Well, not in a formal setting, I'm Lana. And this is Damen," I introduced brightly as I stuck out a hand in greeting.

"You're making a statement with those gloves. I can dig it." Before I could say anything else, she turned to Damen and asked, "Well big guy, what do you want? I can do pretty much anything. Just leave the magic part up to me." She winked at him to add emphasis.

She went on to explain that he could have whatever, and wherever he wanted, even if he wanted it to be invisible. He showed her an image on his phone, and she just smiled.

"Fuck yeah. Step into my office," she agreed, as she escorted us around to a large chair and her official tattooing station.

Addie took some time to set up everything. She made a stencil, placed it on Damen's forearm, and seemed to weave her own brand of magic as she pulled out her inks and got everything ready.

"Do I get to know what you're getting?" I asked Damen.

"No, you can wait," he cooed, pretty much dismissing me.

Groaning, I turned away, respecting his wishes even if it was just to annoy me.

"So Lana, Damen, tell me about yourselves," Addie instructed as she began her assault into Damen's arm. I could hear the telltale buzzing of the tattoo machine.

"Well, I'm basically a what-you-see-is-what-you-get kinda guy. I was gigging and writing music before I was called up to be this one's guardian," he explained. I couldn't see anything but could hear a little pain in his voice. While he'd trained for his position, he too had to leave a life behind.

"What about you, Lana?" Addie asked as the buzzing continued.

"Well, I was almost done with college. I only had one final left. Then I'd have my degree in graphic design. I love to draw and create logos and all kinds of things."

"Hey, that would be useful around here. There are a surprising number of businesses around here. Maybe I can give a nudge in the right direction, I mean if you're up for that kind of thing."

"That would be great!" I nearly cried with excitement.

"And Damen, you should ask Willow at Coffee Haven or Michelle over at Daily Knead, about doing some music days. I can ask around about open mic nights too. Oh snap! There's also Music in the Square on the third Thursdays of the month in the summer. I can send you the details."

"I'd appreciate that."

I thought back to Damen on his guitar and the spell he'd seemed to weave. It would be a shame for the world to be deprived of his talent.

"How are you guys liking our town?" she asked.

"Everyone has been amazingly nice and welcoming. Well, aside from that meeting. It was kind of intense," I admitted, looking at a few photos on the wall.

"Yeah, the Court can be like that at times. But in the end, think of us as a family. A fucking dysfunctional family." She chuckled.

"I believe it," Damen muttered.

"So, Lana, talk to me. You're the new oracle? What's that like?" she asked.

"Well, I can see anyone's future if I touch them. Hence the style choice." I wiggled my fingers.

"Ah."

"But honestly, I don't know what I'm doing. I feel like I've been thrust into this whole thing and I'm just going on fumes." My voice cracked but I refuse to let it take me over.

"Yeah, we've all been there. Even though we might have grown up knowing what we were, we all have times where we are trying to find out what's unique about ourselves and how to be us. Life isn't a straight line. We all have to find our own path."

I hadn't expected such insight from someone my age, but her words caused me to pause for a long moment.

"Well, I'm done here. And if I do say so myself, it's pretty fucking awesome," she announced confidently.

"Can I see?" I chirped, bouncing on my toes.

"It looks good. Fine, oracle, come and see." He sighed as if I'd asked him a million times.

Turning, I saw Addie with her arms crossed, beaming with pride. Damen held his arm out, and I was able to see the image. I froze, unable to formulate a response.

"Do you not like it?" Addie asked in a worried tone.

"Lana?" Damen hedged. After a long moment, I met his gaze.

"You wouldn't believe me unless I showed you," I intoned.

I slid my hands down to my jeans and unbuttoned them. Pulling down the waistline, I exposed the only other tattoo on my body. Silence fell in the small room as we all just looked.

When I turned eighteen, I got a small tattoo on my left hip. It was a Delphian epsilon sitting on the sun. It looked like two curved "E's" that were a mirror image and a line separating them. It was the symbol of Apollo, the god of music and poetry, from whom it was thought that my new power came.

Sitting freshly inked on Damen's arm was the same symbol. While the art differed, as they were done by two different artists, the symbol was just the same.

"Well, that isn't the weirdest shit I've ever seen, but it's pretty far up there," Addie said.

"I guess I don't have to hunt for that tattoo now. But yeah, that's weird as hell," Damen joked.

"Well, if there's nothing else, I have some things to do. And I hear you have a ghost tour to get to," Addie added.

"I hear that as well. Thanks a ton for everything, and I hope we get to hear from you soon about some open mic nights," Damen reminded her as he shook her hand.

"I'm on it! Oh, Lana, I almost forgot. Here's my number." She handed me a card. "Call me for lunch or something. I might have some personal work we could collaborate on."

"I'd love that!" I was excited by the prospect of a friend. I had the feeling Addie would be a good one to hang out with. Hey, I was always down for a friend; I could use all the help I could get at this point.

"So, you're really set to go on this tour, aren't you?" Damen grumbled as we walked down the sidewalk.

"Yes. Come on, you'll have fun!" I gushed brightly, practically dragging him along.

"It's just so touristy," he groaned, as if in pain. I rolled my eyes. I mean, I really couldn't help it. He was being an infant.

"Well, sorry, big guy. We're going! Maybe there will be a stop at a bar, and you can get a beer. Will that make you happy?" I snickered in a tone I'd use with children.

Narrowing his eyes at me, he poked me in the ribs. I yelped and slapped at his hand.

"Hey! That tickled!"

"That's the point, oracle."

We walked along the center square until we came upon a small white trolley. On the side were the words *Moon Light Ghost Tours*. From what I could see, there were only about ten people on the bus, which made me feel better. Less chance of accidently bumping into someone.

We walked up to the bus where a tall dark-haired man, dressed head to toe in black, stood leaning against the white metal.

His gaze shifted to mine, and I had to stifle a gasp. His eyes were like nothing I'd ever seen before. The whole of his right eye was black. It looked as though it had been dipped in black ink. His left eye was a rich sapphire blue.

His grin was the kind of smile that under most circumstances would have had me dropping trow. Now, however, cock-blocking Damen was still complaining behind me.

"Why, hello there." The too-hot-for-his-own-good man seemed to roll the words more than speak them.

"Hi!" I replied, sticking out my glove-clad hand.

Glancing down at it, he smirked.

"Fashion statement?" He took my hand in his.

"Something like that," I joked.

He raised the back of my hand to his lips and placed a soft kiss on it. I felt blood rush to my face and knew I was blushing.

"And what's your name, beautiful girl?" His mouth was still so close to my hand, I could feel his words through the thin leather of the glove.

"Lana," Damen spat from behind us. Somehow the damn brute managed to make my name sound like a curse word. I had no idea what had gotten into him.

Still holding my hand in his, the man flicked his eyes behind me. Whatever he saw caused him to smile in what I would call a challenge.

"Lana, beautiful name. I'm Rayonus. Please call me Ray. I will be your tour guide. Do you happen to have your ticket? Or will you be paying me directly?" He released my hand. The way he said the word *directly* made it sound like a naughty proposition. His little wink didn't help his case in the slightest. Or did it?

Nodding and absolutely not blushing, I handed him our two tickets.

Pushing his way past me, Damen shoved me over and took my place. I let out a little huff and glared at him.

"I'm Damen. And, personally, I think it's far prettier a name." He spat the words as he stuck his hand out.

Ray took the hand and shook it. They both stood there just shaking hands. Something, I wasn't sure what, passed between the two, but the macho-ness of it went way above my pay grade.

"Okay, not that this is awkward or anything, but I'm getting on the bus." I rolled my eyes at their shenanigans as I went up the stairs.

I found a seat up front, next to the window, and sat down. A moment later Damen walked in and sat next to me, of course.

"What the hell was that about?" I hissed in a low tone.

"Nothing. Just didn't like how he looked at you," he grumbled.

Turning in my seat slightly, I crossed my arms over my chest and looked at his sandy brown eyes.

"Damen, we're stuck together for like ever. We have to find some common ground here. I will get hit on. I'll even date. You cannot scare away anyone who wants to come into the same zip code as me."

"It's my job to protect you." He crossed his arms, looking bored.

"I know, but don't protect me into submission. I'm a big girl. Let me live a little, okay, grandpa?"

That caused him to erupt into barks of laughter.

Soon, Ray got on to the bus and the tour started.

The trolley stopped and started a number of times in a number of places within the town. If I had thought the place had magic during the day, at night the place seemed to be reborn into something entirely different. Gone was the innocence of the sun. It was replaced by the taunting moon and the trickster stars.

Ray was absolutely mesmerizing as he told the stories about each of the historical sites of the town. He seemed to know all of the juicy bits of every story. It made me wonder just how old he was. I knew people in this town weren't always what they seemed. While he looked to be in his late twenties, possibly early thirties, I knew there was a good chance he was far older.

He used voices, cracked jokes, and was an absolute shameless flirt. I instantly liked him. In the game of fuck, marry, or kill, he'd firmly be in the fuck category. That line of thought had my eyes shifting to

Damen. *What category would he be in?* I'd seen him in nothing but a towel and he had a great body, so the fuck section was possible, but he was also tender and wasn't afraid to show his emotions.

"What?" he blurted.

I just blinked at him, wondering if I'd spoken aloud.

"You're staring at me."

Damn it!

"Oh, sorry," I mumbled.

The trolley slowed to a stop, just as it had done a number of times. This time, however, it wasn't at a store, old home, or even abandoned building, but rather we stopped at a line of dense trees that ran across the southernmost edge of the town. I looked at Ray, who sported a devilish grin. His pink tongue darted out and ran across his lower lip. He was the definition of trouble.

"I know some of you might be confused as to why we stopped here. There are no sordid stories, no murders, and no hauntings to tell you of." He paused for what could only be assumed to be dramatic effect. "However, there is a myth. Now, whether or not you believe it is up to you."

Motioning to the tree line, he began weaving his tale.

"Just beyond these trees, you will find a dirt path. Along this path it's said you'll see the trials of your own life in some fashion. It has been reported that people walking down it have heard the tinkling bells of children's laughter, though no one quite knows why. At the end of the path, you will come upon a small pond." Ray's one black eye seemed to glint in the light of the moon, making it seem as if it too were a star.

"I heard from a man who went on this journey that if you gaze upon yourself in the waters of the still surface of the pond, you can stare directly into the blind eyes of the Fates themselves and see the moment of your death. Now, I don't know how credible this man was, but he said that if you can find the Fates, they will offer you a boon in return. The last I heard of him, he was still in search of the three hags."

The night around us seemed to grow so still that had a single cricket chirped, it could have been heard for a hundred miles. I had no idea how long we all sat there in silence, letting Ray's words echo into the inky darkness. I didn't realize we were moving until we were nearly back to the center of town.

"Well, gentlemen and"—Ray paused, looked at me, and winked—"ladies, that's the end of our tour. I hope you've enjoyed the very real haunts, stories, and ghosts of our fair town. But be careful—you never know what things might be hunting you in the night."

We all started clapping; even Damen joined in. Everyone filed off the trolley, talking about the tales they'd heard and whether or not they should go hunting them.

Passing Ray, I waved a goodbye and turned to go. I felt a hand grab mine. Forgetting about my gloves, I went to yank my hand back but thought better of it. I turned to see Ray on the other end.

"Hey there, Ms. Lana. I hope you enjoyed the tour."

I opened my mouth to assure him I had, but I didn't get the chance, as Damen shoved his way between us.

"Hands off," Damen snarled.

Letting go of my hand, Ray peered around Damen to meet my eyes.

"I don't think your lapdog likes me very much."

"I don't think I like him very much either," I agreed in an annoyed tone.

Damen whirled to face me. His gaze was fixed, and his lips were peeled back slightly.

"I'm here to protect you," he growled between clenched teeth. "What don't you get about that?"

Putting one hand on my hip and the other one gesturing to Ray, I hissed, "Does it look like I need protecting?"

His jaw turned into a white line of strain.

"Yeah, boss, trust me. My intentions are purely"—he paused and licked his lips—"honorable." How he made that word sound utterly sexual was beyond me. That's when I understood. Ray was baiting Damen. And Damen was falling for it. His arms and chest were growing in size. I had to figure out a way to defuse the situation before it became a thing.

I was going to hate myself for how much of an absolute dumb girl I was about to be, but it was all I could think of.

Internally I rolled my eyes, then I stepped off the curb and mock twisted my ankle.

"Oh, ouch!" I complained loudly.

Damen sucked in a breath, fell to his knees, and put his hands on my foot.

"Lana! Are you okay?" he fretted in a worried tone.

Sliding his hands from my foot to my ankle, he inspected the supposed wound.

Ray gave me a knowing smile, winked, and walked away. He was absolutely fuckable, but not a bit marriage material.

Damen slipped his arms under me and lifted me up, cradling me. I was one hundred percent capable of walking, but I let myself sink a little deeper into his hold. Besides, it wasn't like he'd ever know I wasn't really hurt.

CHAPTER 7

J had thought my biggest hurdle to overcome would be getting the Court's approval to renew the compact. Whoo boy, was I wrong!

"Have you even made a dent in it?" Damen wondered, looking over my shoulder at the illuminated screen.

I let out a huge breath and pinched my brow in frustration. He was referring to my petitioner list. I'd been in Havenwood Falls five days before I started seeing people, and that had been two weeks ago. I wasn't even close to catching up to the forever long list.

"No." I breathed the word. Staring back at me was the list. The long as hell, hundred-years-long freaking list.

I let my head slump slowly down until I felt it hit the keyboard.

"Could you see more people?" Damen suggested, knowing full well the answer.

"No," I groaned. "I'm pretty wiped out if I see more than five a day. Remember the day we thought we could bump it up to ten?"

As if in answer, I felt his hands touch my shoulders. He brushed his fingers so lightly against my bare shoulders, it was as if his touch was a question. I froze, wondering where he was going. His grip tightened and then loosened. He was massaging my overtired and overworked muscles.

I couldn't help but melt into his hands. I swear someone even started moaning. Oh wait, yeah, that was totally me. I should have stopped him, told him I was fine, told him I could take care of myself. But that would have been a lie. I shouldn't have taken comfort in him, or at least I held some convoluted idea I shouldn't take comfort in a guy I hardly knew.

"You think too much," he whispered. Sometimes I wondered if he shared a little of my powers.

I knew he was right. So in that moment, I just shut my brain off and enjoyed someone else taking care of me. I found myself drifting in and out of consciousness. It felt as if I was falling in a slow cradle-like descent to the ground. But for whatever reason, I wasn't afraid of falling. I fell for what seemed like hours, until I felt something hit me. I opened my eyes and didn't understand what I was seeing. I was standing smack dab in the middle of the Havenwood Falls downtown square, except it was fully night and I couldn't recall how I'd gotten here.

Something zipped past my ear, making a whistling noise as it fell to the ground. I glanced down and saw a glowing red ember. What the—

I had a sinking feeling. Turning around, I sank to my knees and my hand flew to my mouth in horror. Fire was raining down on the town, people were running, and buildings were burning. I tried to scream, but the heat from the building blaze stole my voice away. I couldn't move. I couldn't help as the people tried to drop and roll to put out the fire on their bodies. They were burning. Everything was burning.

This time I was able to scream. This time my voice rang out, shattering everything.

"Lana! Lana!" a voice echoed. I felt myself shaking and sobbing. I was out of control. I thrashed against my restraints, but nothing changed. I was trapped by iron.

"Lana." This time the voice was soft, feather light. It was a pause button to my wild emotions and caused me to still.

Finally, after a long moment, I opened my eyes. Looking back at me was Damen. He suddenly felt like an anchor, something tethering me to the earth, keeping me from flying away.

"You okay?" I rasped. His features were pulled tight and his skin slightly pale.

"Me? You're the one asking if I'm okay? You're a trip," he scoffed, as he ran a hand over my sweat-soaked forehead.

"What happened?" I hesitated. I was a bit confused. I'd had visions, but this was unlike anything I'd ever seen before.

"I was rubbing your shoulders and you fell asleep. I carried you to bed then went to bed myself. I heard you screaming—" His voice cracked slightly, but he coughed as if to hide something. "I tried to wake you up but couldn't. Then you just stopped once I started whispering to you."

I couldn't look at him. I couldn't tell him what I'd seen. Hell, I didn't really even know what I saw.

We both sat there on my bed, him holding me and me letting him. After a while he moved to get up.

"Wait!" I panicked. He froze at my words. He looked down at me, and there was something in his expression that I couldn't name. He seemed to be holding his breath.

I had no idea what possessed me, but I reached up to his face and pulled him down to me. Brushing my lips against his, I felt him tense under my fingertips. What in the gods' names was I thinking? I pulled away. *I'm so dumb!*

Suddenly, he crushed his lips to mine. Gripping his hand in my hair, he tilted my face up to his as if to give himself better access to me. My heart felt as if it would jump out of my chest, it was beating so quickly.

I parted my lips and let him explore me. When I'd kissed Cassie, she'd always been quick to retreat, never taking the time to let us explore one another. But this was so different. It was as if with each lick and each nip he was trying to learn what I liked and what would steal my breath away. I leaned up to him, pushing my chest against his. I couldn't get close enough to him. I wanted to rip our clothes off just so I could feel his skin next to mine. His hand snaked up to my breast, and he found my nipple in short order. I would have sucked in a breath of surprise or even moan in pleasure, but he just swallowed every emotion I had.

Knock knock. We both froze. After ten or so seconds the knocking returned, and with it my brain reengaged.

"You have a night petitioner, don't you?" he huffed, breathlessly.

I nodded as he dropped his hands from me. They fell onto his lap with a disappointing slap.

"I forgot." I panted.

Getting up, Damen walked to the door. I couldn't help but notice his slight shift in the groin area. Nor could I help the smirk plastered on my face.

Just before he walked out of the room, he intoned, "Don't think this is over, oracle."

My smile faltered, and heat flooded my whole body. Now it was him not trying to hide his smirk.

"Come on, you have a petitioner." He laughed half-heartedly as he offered his hand to me.

Getting off the bed, I took the hand he'd stuck out.

I paused, causing him to look back at me.

"Is that a promise?" I flirted huskily.

In answer, he just squeezed my hand and pulled me to the door. I had no damn idea how I was going to get through this without him distracting me, but I had to. Then there was that dream. I'd never seen anything like it before, but I had a bad gut feeling that it meant something. Trouble was, I didn't know what.

I walked into the front room and sat down. I gave Damen a nod, and he opened the door.

"Hello and welcome to the home of the sacred oracle. While I understand you might have your own rules, I will have to ask a few things. First, all weapons must be left outside. This is a home of neutral territory. Any acts of violence toward the oracle will be dealt with swiftly. Second, no shifting, use of magic, or biting of any kind. Leave your bad attitudes at the door. And last, while the oracle is a gift to all beings from the gods of old, she will never ask for payment. I, however, as her guardian, ask that you make an offering. Just remember, we have to eat," Damen explained to my last visitor of the day. I'd heard this same spiel a number of times. While it varied here and there, the intent was nearly always the same.

"I understand and accept your terms," a rumbling male voice sounded.

Metal clanged against concrete, leading me to believe that some kind of weapon had been dropped on the floor.

A tall thin man with salt-and-pepper hair rounded the corner. He had sharp features that looked as though he'd been carved by someone who shouldn't have given up their day job.

Standing up, I stuck out my newly gloved hand in greeting. "Hello, Mr. Roth. I'm Lana."

He scowled at me for a moment but took my hand. He grimaced as if I'd been covered in garbage. *Well, this is going to go swimmingly, I can just tell. Ugh.*

"Thank you for seeing me. I only had to wait seventy-three years, three weeks, and five days. The last two weeks and five days being past my scheduled time." If a voice could sound both oily and pissed the fuck off, his did.

Damen stepped a little closer to me as if he was warning the man.

"I am sorry for that. But as I explained on the phone, the last oracle died, and I had just come into the power. I needed the time to get my life situated so I could see petitioners as soon as possible," I added, my own irritation showing, and I didn't feel a bit bad about it.

"Excuses aren't very becoming for a new oracle," Roth snapped.

"Sir, the oracle has been very patient with you, but I won't be. If you continue to be rude, you'll be asked to leave without what you came here for," Damen said in a cool and dispassionate tone.

The man's deep black eyes flashed a red color, but nothing else gave away a single emotion.

"I'm sorry," the man finally groused, though his words were empty. The man blinked as he looked around the room. I could nearly hear his judgment through his disgusted look. *Yeah, well, you and me both, buddy,* I didn't say in reference to the creepy-as-fuck dolls. I should probably do something with them, but I never seemed to have my motivation and time line up.

I slid my glove off and looked at him fully. I knew nothing about the man other than his name. I didn't know what race, breed, or creed he was; I liked it that way.

"I have no control over what I see. Anything I tell you is the truth. Anything I see will not be disclosed to anyone other than you. These are my vows, and I take them seriously." He nodded at my words. "Please feel free to visit the town of Havenwood Falls. But please follow the rules that have been emailed to you prior," I added.

He again nodded.

I removed my glove, reached out, and requested, "May I have your hand, Mr. Roth?"

He placed his cold hand within mine.

Warmth spread throughout my body, and I sank into my vision.

Roth sat in a large red velvet chair. Crackling and snapping of burning logs came from somewhere behind him. The glow of the fire cast everything in a flickering amber hue.

At his feet lay a crumpled mess of cloth and pale skin. Roth sipped at his drink for a moment before setting it aside. His attention never left the bloody body at his feet, despite his best efforts.

Taking in a deep breath, he kneeled by the corpse, grabbed a handful of hair, and angled her face up to his. He lovingly brushed the woman's dark hair from her face, leaving smears of blood streaking across her pale skin.

"Oh, daughter mine. You'll forgive me for this one day. On the day when I meet you at the gates of hell." His voice was soft and echoed a deep-set pain.

I gasped for air and blinked rapidly, hoping for my vision to return. After a few hard blinks, everything came into focus.

"Well? What did you see?" Roth demanded impatiently.

I'd only been seeing petitioners for a short time, but this one had shaken me to my core. I glanced over to Damen, who studied me. I tried to convey my worry to him, but wasn't sure he picked up on it.

Taking a deep breath, I explained everything in great detail. Roth bombarded me with three hundred questions. I did my best to answer him, but with each one, he seemed to get more and more irate.

"Who killed her?" he huffed for the third time.

"Mr. Roth, I don't know. I saw no one else in the vision but you and her."

"Are you saying I killed her?" His fists slammed down on the table.

Damen stepped forward and grabbed the man by the wrist.

Yanking Roth off his seat and to his feet, Damen explained in a cool tone, "And your time is up. If you have an offering, leave it on the doorstep." From the way Damen's outline swelled and how tight his clothes grew, I knew he took this threat deadly seriously.

"Let. Go. Of. Me," the man huffed, doing some yanking of his own. Damen didn't let the man go until he'd made it perfectly clear that he—and he alone—controlled the situation. Once free of Damen's grip and outside the door, he turned to face the small home and brushed his clothes off.

I walked over to the door and stood just behind Damen. The tall man met my eyes for a long moment before turning and walking away. I could feel Damen's rage coming off him in waves.

Shutting the door and turning around, Damen mumbled, "Asshole."

Maybe it had been the dream I'd had, the vision, the rude guy, or even the kiss, but the enormity of everything began to hit me all at once.

I gave up everything to do a job I knew nothing about. I read journal after journal explaining the laws as set forth by my gods, and now I was faced with people constantly using me. I was nothing more than a tool. For what exactly? For people to treat me like I owed them something?

"Why do people feel like they can use me and then toss me out like garbage? Like I'm not even a person." I realized only after I'd spoken that the words had come out loud. I could feel myself slipping down a rabbit hole of loss. I was losing myself and letting the oracle take over. Maybe this was how it was supposed to be? I was granted this power to be of use, nothing more?

"Lana—" Damen started. But my hand flew up, stopping him.

"Damen, I don't want your pity," I snapped, and immediately regretted it. "I'm sorry."

"No, I get it. That guy was an ass and you feel used."

I wished that was all. I wished I could be more like him. He'd been preparing for this role his whole life. All the while I'd been running from it.

"I just want to go to sleep." It was late, and I just wanted to forget that guy. I just wanted to forget everything. I just hoped I could find my place, find my reason and stop feeling like something to be used.

"Okay, well I'll see you in—"

"Wait! I want you to sleep with me," I blurted out. As if it could have somehow shoved the words back in, my hand flew up to my mouth.

He cocked an eyebrow at me, and his expression of worry was replaced by one of intrigue.

"Well, I thought you'd never ask," he crooned as he waggled his eyebrows. Those poor caterpillars were getting the workout of their lives.

"No, I mean, uh, I want you to just be there. Not like anything, uh, um." I stammered. I couldn't seem to get the words out.

Chuckling lightly, he softly grabbed my hand and led me to my room.

"Come on, oracle. Let me protect you while you sleep."

And as though his words had a direct line to my stomach, butterflies once again erupted in a panic.

After slipping into my grungy shorts and my three-sizes-too-big top, I crawled into bed. I was drained and after that last guy, I just wanted to close my eyes and sink into sleep.

"What's your favorite food?" Damen puzzled as he sank into the spot next to me. This should have been awkward or at least felt somewhat wrong, but it didn't, and that fact alone should have scared the shit out of me.

"Coffee." I yawned.

"I know you want to work hard to get caught up, but how about we go get some tomorrow? We have an hour break. It would be nice to do something different."

I opened my mouth to reply, but Hades let out a loud meow and hopped onto the bed. The white cat circled a few times, trying to find a spot. Once he realized his normal place was taken, he looked at Damen and hissed.

"There's something wrong with that damn cat." Damen sighed.

"You're not wrong," I agreed, as Hades curled up in the small space above my head.

"Let's worry about tomorrow, tomorrow," I yawned sleepily. As much as I wanted to be positive and embrace all of these changes, I didn't know how much more I could take.

Slowly, I let my mind clear and sank into a dream-filled sleep.

CHAPTER 8

*C*offee Haven was located on the south side of the town square and, in my opinion, was one of the most unique spots in the whole town.

"Wow," I breathed, looking up at the menu. They had everything from herbal teas to specialty lattes and every snack in between.

"I still think we need to go back home. I can't believe you forgot your gloves." Damen sounded like a disapproving brother—well, what I assumed one would have sounded like.

"I'll be careful. Plus, I need coffee," I whined as I stuck out my bottom lip.

"It's noon, Lana," he moaned as he playfully tugged on my pouted lip.

"And I need coffee. I fail to see how the time affects whether I should have coffee. What's the saying? It's five o'clock somewhere?" I explained indignantly.

"I'm not too sure that's how it works."

Was I in a cinnamon mood or caramel? Hmmm.

A little voice screamed, causing me to turn around. It happened so fast, I didn't even have time to think about my reactions. A little boy no more than five came directly at me, his soft red hair floating in a crown of flames as he flew toward me. He was looking back at his mother, or the woman I assumed to be his mother, who was chasing after him. However, he was paying far more attention to the little girl with silver white hair who was toddling after him. The little girl let out a joyful shriek of excitement.

"Jacob, Arabella, look out!" the woman with bright red hair called. The little boy ran smack into me and bounced against my leg to the floor with an audible thud. And in short order the little girl followed, tripping over the pile of little boy.

I couldn't hide the grimace on my face as the little one looked up at me. Like flipping a switch, he started crying, alligator tears and all. Arabella looked from me to him and back again, then she too broke out into tears.

"Aw, babies, it's okay." I bent down and tried to reassure them. Without warning, Jacob launched himself at me, wrapping his arms around my neck. Arabella just sat on the floor, still crying. A thin woman with the same light blond hair as the little girl, who'd been standing with the other woman, walked over to the crying girl.

"Arabella, it's okay, love. You should know better than to play tag with Jacob inside the shop." Meeting my gaze, she smiled a shy smile and added, "Sorry, they don't get a lot of time together. I'm Willow Fairchild. This little one is Arabella. You've already met Jacob, and his aunt Aster McCabe is just over there." She pointed to a red-haired woman who was walking over.

"It's totally fine! I just hope they're okay," I said as the little boy still hugged me.

"Jacob, you're fine, buddy! Let go of the poor woman." Aster chuckled as her green eyes squinted in a half smile.

Jacob relaxed slightly, allowing me to release him. He gave me a crooked smile framed by a dusting of adorable freckles. The little boy slid his small warm hand into mine, and that's when I realized my mistake. Images of the little boy's future took me over.

Wild and floating fire red hair sprung to life as the little boy jumped from one foot to the other as he munched on a sugar cookie in the shape of a purple flower. In his other hand, the boy gripped a napkin tightly.

"Jacob, come on, come get my hand," his aunt called after him. Her

bright green eyes peered at her nephew, so full of love and a fierce protectiveness.

However, a strong gust of wind snatched the napkin from Jacob's hand and sent it flying into the busy street. Without thinking, the boy went running after it. Neither he nor his aunt saw the blue SUV coming.

He lay on the ground bleeding, his once lively fiery hair lifeless and his expression no longer full of joy and energy. His aunt let out a scream so loud that if emotion alone could have kept that little boy tied to this earth, hers would have.

Time was irrelevant; a surge of people ran to help as the little boy lay still on the pavement. His cookie was still clutched in his tiny lifeless hand.

I gasped for air, clutching the small child's hand in mine. I could feel the heated streaks of tears that were streaming down my face.

"You okay, Jacob?" his aunt said cautiously. It was then I realized how strange the scene must have looked. I was grasping her nephew's hand tightly and glowing. Thank god it was daytime and my glow was harder to see.

I let the boy go, and he went running to his aunt. Wiping his face clean of tears, Aster placed a small kiss on the tip of his nose.

"Come on, let's get you a cookie. We have purple flowers today. I bet if you're really good, we can talk Willow into giving you one while we visit!"

My heart sank at her words. I hadn't seen too far into the future because he had none.

"Willow! Don't you know a day off means a day off? As in, you don't need to come in?" the shaggy-haired man behind the counter joked, sporting a crooked grin and fixing his thick black rimmed glasses. Looking to Aster, he added, "Always good to see you, Aster. You're missed around here and left some big shoes for me to fill."

"Lana," Damen whispered in my ear, "you saw something, didn't you?"

I could only nod as I watched the two women with the children approach the marble countertop and talk with the man behind the counter.

"He's about to die." I nearly choked on the whispered words.

"Fuck. Lana, don't do something stupid," he spat.

I knew what he meant. I couldn't actually say anything. I was bound by the laws of the gods. If he wasn't on my list, I could not affect his future. But how could I possibly sit back and do nothing? How could I watch him die twice?

The words my ya-ya had written flashed in my mind. *They will not hesitate to rain hell on earth should you break a sacred law.* Had that been what that weird dream was about? But why was it a law? Who made these laws? Well, other than the gods themselves.

The little boy's clothes were the same, the cookie was the same, and his aunt handed him a small white napkin. How? How could I be asked to do nothing? How could I be expected to sit back and watch a child die?

"Damen . . ." I intoned.

"Lana, don't do this." There was resignation in his tone. I think, in some way, he knew I didn't have a choice.

"Damen, what choice do I have? I can't let him die," I whispered.

I met Willow's aqua-colored eyes for a moment. Her brow was pinched, her expression drawn. I didn't know her, but for whatever reason, she seemed to react to my fears and worry. However, just when I thought she'd say something, she turned and gave Aster a hug and cupped Jacob's freckle-filled cheek.

Jacob and Aster were leaving the store. I didn't have much time to make this choice. This was a sacred law; this was one they would punish the hell out of me for. I glanced at the little boy's bright copper hair and how it seemed to be full of just as much life as he was. I could never forget his small hand gripping that cookie.

The door shut as the pair walked out of the coffee shop. I was officially out of time.

Without further thought, I raced after them. Swinging the door open, I looked to the right, but saw nothing. Then I looked to the left and spotted the little boy balancing on a curb. I froze, giving what I was doing a second thought. The napkin flew out of his hand and into the street.

I went as fast as my feet could carry me. I glanced at the oncoming car. I'd waited too long. I wouldn't get there in time. A strong gust of wind blew by me, causing my hair to fall over my face. Clearing it, my eyes went wild looking for the boy who I just knew would be— The sound of screeching tires caused my heart to skip a beat.

"No!" I screamed in horror. I rushed over to the small crowd of people who'd gathered to see—nothing but a crushed cookie on the ground. Just beyond the car knelt a panting Damen, who cradled a small figure with fluttering red hair.

"That man just came out of nowhere. If—if he hadn't been there, Jacob would have been hit!" Willow gasped right next to me.

Meeting my tear-filled gaze, she breathed, "You?"

I blinked, and a tear rolled down my cheek. I couldn't speak. I just couldn't formulate the words. She knew. I didn't know how, but she did. I ran over to the other side of the street, where Damen sat hushing the scared little boy. His aunt ran over only moments before I had. He'd done it even when he'd told me not to. He knew just as much as I did what this meant. But why?

"Jacob!" Aster screamed.

Letting the boy go, Damen made his way to his feet. I ran full force at him, and like I knew he would, he caught me just as I jumped at him. I didn't even try to hide the sob that escaped my lips.

"Shh," he crooned reassuringly, as he rubbed his big protective hand against my back.

"Why?" I croaked. I was not a pretty crier, so I was grateful my face was buried in his shoulder.

Running his hand through my hair, he whispered, "You were right. I couldn't stand back and do nothing. So whatever the punishment is, we're in it together."

And the snot-pouring, hiccup-producing, slobber-dripping sobs took me over.

"Wow, I can tell you're an ugly-ass crier," he joked.

I tried to laugh, but it only came out a gurgling mess of unintelligible sounds.

"Come on, oracle, let's go home and figure out how to hide from a bunch of old Greek gods."

He set me down, and I ran a sleeve over my runny nose. Looking over my shoulder, I saw Jacob and Aster walking toward us.

"I—" Aster started but was cut off by a small sob. Her delicate features were pulled taut with what I was sure was a mix of fear, relief, and everything in between. Her pale skin and green eyes seemed to stand out more with her extreme emotions. Getting herself under control, she tried again, "I cannot thank you enough; you . . . you saved Jacob." Glancing at me, she seemed to ask me if it was okay. I simply smiled in agreement. She threw her arms around Damen with Jacob still tightly clutched in her arms.

"Ma'am, no need to thank me. I was just in the right place at the right time."

My heart swelled at his words. I was so proud of him.

"I—I used to work here." She gestured toward the coffee shop before adding, "Please, if you ever need anything, anything at all, don't hesitate to ask for help. Gosh, I didn't even get your names. And I'm totally rambling."

"I'm Damen and this is Lana. We're new to town," he replied, his voice wavering slightly. His body shifted back and forth. I blinked as I realized he didn't like being the center of attention. And in that moment, I decided he was firmly in the marry category. Okay, marry and fuck.

"Well, I'm glad you're here! I mean, not just because of this. Oh man, I just can't thank you enough. I don't know what I'd do without him! I, just, his dad, my brother—" Her words broke off as tears began streaming down her flushed cheeks. She hugged the little boy tightly to her chest.

"Aunt Aster. I can't. Breathe!" the little boy croaked.

Releasing her hold on him, she bent down so that she met the little boy's eyes on his level.

"Jacob, I love you. I wouldn't be able to live with myself if something happened to you." She pulled the boy to her and sobbed into his rust-colored hair. Willow ran over, her little girl in tow. She threw her arms around Aster and Jacob but met my eyes.

With tears in her own eyes, Willow mouthed, "Thank you," to me, not Damen. She knew. Whatever doubt I held, it was utterly quashed in that moment.

A bright flash of light was followed shortly by two immensely loud cracks that brought my hands up to cover my ears. The sound caused me to sink to my knees. I actually had to pull my hands from my ears to be sure I wasn't bleeding. Everyone who'd been gathered in the square scattered to avoid the sudden turn of the weather. I, however, knew better. That wasn't the lightning of an impending thunderstorm. Rather it was the warning of an angry god or gods. A flash of fire raining down covered my vision, but when I blinked, there was nothing but the street and square.

Damen and I locked eyes and blurted at the same time, "We need to go."

All I could think about on the way back to our little cabin was how I was going to talk my way out of this one. One thing I knew for sure was I would be taking the fall for this. No matter what it was, it wouldn't be Damen. It was my fault, not his. I forgot my gloves, I took the risk, and I failed.

"Damen," I sighed.

"Oh, no you don't. You aren't taking the blame for this. I'm a big boy. I can make my own mistakes. I can pull up my own big boy panties."

"How'd you know? Wait, panties?" I stammered as we walked into the house. Did he just say panties? Did he wear them? Oh, I hoped not.

"It's written all over your face. I could see you plotting in the car, and knowing you, you were devising some plan to take the fall. And more the metaphorical panties, not literal."

"Well, if I hadn't forgotten my gloves . . . had I just listened to you and gone back, we wouldn't be in this mess." I sighed.

Walking slowly over to me, he slid his hand behind my head and tilted my face to his.

"Yes, but then Jacob would be dead. And, oracle, I deem that as a worthy fuckup," he said, just before lowering his lips to mine.

What had started as a soft kiss quickly turned into something more frantic. He cupped my ass so firmly against him that I could feel the hard press of his erection against my belly.

As if I'd done it a million times before, I hopped up and wrapped my legs around him. I ground my hips against his in search of friction —fuck, anything more. He in turn grabbed my ass harder and held me as though I belonged there. We fit. It was actually a little scary with how well we fit together. He stumbled backward for a second, but then walked his way through the small home to my bedroom.

I couldn't seem to stop myself from kissing him. From nibbling his full bottom lip. From rubbing myself against him, praying for some feel of his skin, his cock, anything.

Breaking our kiss mid-nip, he groaned. "Fuck, girl, if you keep grinding on me like that, I'm going to have a mess to clean up before we really get this show on the road." *Now, there's a thought.*

My face must have shown how intriguing I thought that idea was because he dropped me on the bed so hard, I nearly bounced off the other side.

I let out a little huff as I landed. Suddenly, he grabbed either side of my favorite Cowboy Bebop shirt and ripped it down the center as if it'd been made of tissue paper.

Looking down at myself, then back up at him, I crooned, "Did you just . . . ?"

Giving me a wicked grin, he replied, "Yeah, I totally did." He then tossed off his shirt and threw it to the floor.

By Hades's bouncing balls, his body was the real gift from the gods. Every single move he made, whether it was twisting or simply breathing, seemed to cause every muscle to ripple. It was like a kaleidoscope of strength the way his body moved. After the last however many years that I'd been strictly dating women, looking at him made me remember how attractive the human form could be, male or female.

It was then I realized that he was looking at me with about as much awe as I was looking at him. I couldn't help but feel a little self-conscious. I went to cover up my exposed flesh.

"Don't you dare," he snarled in warning. "Just let me look at you." He licked his lips and kept on staring. I felt like his meal.

Feeling suddenly bold, I arched my back up and un-hooked my bra. I slid the lacy material off, leaving myself topless. He didn't move a muscle, only his eyes tracking me.

"Damn, woman," he hissed, as if in pain. However, I knew better.

Leaning down, he pressed his mouth to my collarbone and placed a small kiss on the skin, leaving gooseflesh in his wake. He trailed his soft kisses all along my chest before pausing just above my nipple. He didn't move, but he was so close, I could feel his warm breath teasing me. *Oh, fuck this.* I arched up at him, brushing the pebbled flesh against his lips.

Slipping a hand beneath my back, he pulled my nipple into his mouth. Heat exploded throughout my whole body, and a moan escaped my lips.

Without my permission, my hips bucked up, searching for some kind of friction.

"Need something?" he teased, before returning his mouth to my other nipple. He was playing with me, taunting me.

"Please." I wasn't above begging or guiding him to what I needed.

My nipple still in his mouth, he moved his hand from under me to the waistband of my pants and flicked the button open.

"Thanks for not ripping these. I really like them," I breathed.

He released the suction he had on me and raised an eyebrow.

"I could change that, ya know," he threatened in a deep rumbling tone.

However, he pulled my jeans off me and tossed them over his shoulder. All that lay between him and my complete nudity was a small scrap of black lace.

Sitting back on his heels, he looked down at me and sighed, "Fuck me."

Raising an eyebrow, I purred, "I plan on it."

I leaned up and ran my fingers along every bump and valley his gracious body was made of. Meeting his eyes, I flicked open the button on his jeans. That tiny movement caused such a big man to suck in a breath. *Is he trembling under my fingertips?*

I let a finger slide a little further south and— His hand grabbed mine as I felt the head of him press lightly against my finger. Holy gods, I hadn't expected that. He had to be big, really big.

"Oh god!" I whispered as my eyes went wide.

"I've been called a lot of things. God I'm okay with," he joked in a cocky tone.

"No, I just—I could get pregnant. Um, I mean do you have a—a condom?" I hadn't had to think about that kind of thing lately, as my last two relationships had been with women.

"Oh, uh yeah, I thought, never mind. Yeah, I got it covered." Something, I couldn't name what, flashed across his face, but just as I thought I'd seen it, he leaned in and kissed me full on the mouth. Sliding my hand down further, I unzipped him, and his pants fell to the floor.

My eyes went wide at the sight of him. Oh holy night, that thing was just—just too much. There was no possibility on the planet I could even contemplate doing anything with that weapon.

"You're staring at me," he pointed out nervously.

"Oh, sorry," I mumbled, pulling him on top of me.

The press of our naked bodies lit a fire deep within me, one that I'd never really experienced before. Every inch of my body needed him, the press of his heated skin, the lap of his wet tongue, even the bite of his teeth. Now it was I who was starving.

He kissed me, taking in my taste and learning how I liked to be touched. He took his time allowing me to become accustomed to both how I wanted him to touch me and how he wanted to touch.

With every stroke of his fingers and caress of his taut silken skin, he was stoking a fire deep inside me that only grew in intensity. I'd never been so wet in my life. He was driving me out of my mind with need.

"I can't take this anymore." I moaned as his fingers dipped low to cup my sex in his heated hand.

"Shh, I know. I'm going to give you the world." He kissed me lightly.

Suddenly, he got off the bed. It had been the first time ever in my life that someone's absence left me feeling hollow and unfulfilled. I knew in that second that whatever was blooming between us was unlike anything I'd ever experienced.

He appeared again at the foot of the bed and crawled his way up my body one painful inch at a time. He paused at my core. Spreading me open with one hand, he took one long lick of me. We both moaned in approval. He licked again, and again. And I was being pushed to my peak. I was being hurtled toward a precipice one lick at a time, and I wanted nothing more than to dive off headfirst.

Likely knowing I was close, he stopped. I moaned in protest, as I'd been so damn close. But he just kissed his way up my body until he came to my lips.

"Do you want me to wipe my—" I cut his words off, my lips devouring his mouth.

I let my tongue explore him. It darted in and out of his so much like the sex act that I had to let out a moan.

He broke the kiss and gazed down at me.

"I like the way you taste," he breathed.

"I like the way I taste on your lips," I added breathlessly.

"Fuck, that's sexy." He growled as he pressed himself against me.

I lay back and let my legs fall open around him in both supplication and invitation.

He leaned back, and I heard the rustling of a foil packet. A moment later he hovered over me.

I needed him. I needed him and everything that went along with being with him.

He rubbed himself along my folds, allowing himself to breach me for only a moment before retreating and starting over again. It was maddening, this rhythm he was building, then tearing down.

"Please," I pleaded.

He laughed a strained, almost pain-filled laugh. That's when I realized his need was just as strong as mine. It wasn't just in his laugh, but the pull of his lips and the focus of his light brown eyes.

This time when he breached me, he didn't move away. He slid in a little bit. My hands flew to his shoulders, and my eyes went wide.

"Did I hurt you?" he panted, his voice full of fear.

"No, just go slow. It's been a long time since I've been with a man." I couldn't help but be a little afraid.

Giving me a soft, knowing smile, he kissed the tip of my nose before rocking a little more inside of me. I gasped at the pain.

He reached down and found my clit in short order. He began rubbing the sensitive flesh with slow careful circles. A rush of heat and wetness surged through me. My body responded to his, welcoming him as he was able to slide further in. Any time I'd start to feel pain, he allowed my body to get something it needed to take in more. He played my body as if he'd known it for a hundred years, as if I was his instrument and he'd trained his whole life for this moment. After a few more strokes, he was buried deep in me.

Sweat began to bead up on his forehead, and his whole body trembled lightly. He wasn't moving; he was just there, looking down at me. I realized he was waiting on me to move.

Grabbing his hips, I began to move with him. He followed the pace I set. After a while, I was matching him stroke for stroke. I could feel my release building up to a fever pitch, waiting for that last spark before I flew apart into a million and one pieces of the old me I used to be.

"I . . ." I let the statement hang, unable to get the words out.

"I know." He seemed to understand that talking was an action I wasn't able to perform at the moment.

He plunged so deep within me that if I'd had a voice left, I would have screamed his name. I would have praised the gods for this moment. That was all it took to send me headlong into a soul-fracturing orgasm.

I could feel my pleasure pulsing, dragging him deeper into me. He shuddered against me as his orgasm overtook him. His rhythm became frantic, but his eyes never left mine. It was this connection that went further than sex, deeper than conversation. It was a feeling of a deep forever.

He collapsed on top of me, causing the little air I'd managed to suck in to whoosh right back out.

Hitting his shoulder, I croaked, "You're too big. I can't breathe!"

"That's what she said! OH AH!" He laughed before rolling over.

As much as I didn't want to laugh, I couldn't help it.

We both lay there for a long moment, basking in the afterglow of simply being with one another.

Finally, he got up, went to the bathroom and cleaned up. Once he returned, I did the same.

"I'm ready for bed. Thank the gods we don't have any more petitioners today." I yawned as I fell back into the soft mattress.

"Same. You wore me out today. Between saving kids, coffee, and other things." There was a smile of satisfaction plastered so big on his face, it could have been its own billboard.

"Oh, you loved it!" I huffed as I smacked his shoulder.

"Well, I know I enjoyed the show," a deep, rumbling male voice intoned. My heart nearly stopped at the sound of someone new in the room.

CHAPTER 9

*D*amen bolted to his feet, still on the bed, and still nude as the day he was born. While that thing could have been registered as a deadly weapon, I doubted it was going to be his best choice, in the moment. However, it did swing in the air like a pendulum.

"Stand down, guardian. I mean no harm to your oracle," ordered the man, whom I'd still not seen.

There was something in his voice. I knew I hadn't heard it before, but there was something deep within me that stirred at the sound of it.

"No" was all Damen warned.

A glowing blue light began to fill the room, like someone had put a light on a dimmer switch and began turning it. It was then I saw a man sitting in the black leather chair in the corner. He was a thin, lanky man with wild black hair and skin that looked somehow paler than milk. His eyes, though—they weren't an ice blue; oh no, nothing about this man, er, being was cold. His eyes were the same blue as the hottest part of a flame, and if I had to venture a guess, just as deadly. He was dressed in a tight-fitting suit, so tight in fact that I would be willing to bet that if he got a hard on, his pants would rip right in half.

At that moment, my damn cat jumped up on the strange man's suit-clad lap, turning around three times and settling down.

"Hades!" I hissed.

The cat looked at me with what could only be described as a *What?* expression.

At the same time, the man smiled a dangerous smile and also replied, "Yes?"

My eyes went wide, and not just at the sight of Damen's full moon.

"How about your guardian gets some clothes on and we all sit down for a little chat," the man I really hoped wasn't *the* Hades advised in an amused tone. And then he just disappeared. I don't mean that he ran so damn fast he looked like he'd just disappeared—no, he actually *poofed* gone. The cat looked just as stunned as I felt.

Damen just stood there while I still clutched the sheet to my chest. We both gawked at the space the stranger had just occupied a moment before.

"You don't think he's really . . ." I let the statement hang in the air as the whole disbelief of the situation dawned on me.

"Yeah, oracle, I really do." Damen sighed as he got off the bed and pulled his pants on.

As we walked into the living room, hand in hand, my heart felt like it was going to burst right through my chest and plummet to the floor. I had to stifle a gasp at the sight of the foreign man sitting on my sofa. *Was he reading my mail?*

"Hey!" I chided. I then thought better of it. Yeah, scolding a bazillion-year-old god, wonderful plan, said no one ever.

"Hello, oracle and her guardian," he replied, with absolutely no inflection in his tone at all. It was actually a little eerie.

"Uh, hi?" It came out more of a question rather than a statement.

"Come have a seat," he suggested, motioning to my couch. I had no idea why, but I was discomfited by the fact that he was inviting me to sit on my own damn furniture. However, I thought better of pushing my luck with the god of the underworld. For once I thought better of talking back. Yay, go me.

Damen and I did as instructed. The three of us sat in my living room just looking at one another, surrounded by creepy dolls. Well wasn't this exactly how every single horror movie ever started out? Ugh, I swore I wouldn't be the first one dead.

Hades opened his mouth to say something, but my cat took that as his cue to make his presence known yet again. Hades the cat jumped up on the coffee table and let out the absolute loudest meow I'd ever heard. He then walked over to Hades the god to inspect the newcomer.

The god of the underworld leaned in with his hand extended to let the feline take a sniff. My cat, the fickle being he was, hissed, did a slow turn around, waved his butt in the air, and jumped off the table.

"By Zeus's cock, that cat has the biggest balls I've ever seen!" The god eyed the cat as he sauntered off.

"Yeah, I got him fixed, but he was depressed afterward, so I had them put those fake ones in, you know, the neuticle things. Anyway, long story short, it was the wrong size, and he's now super confident. It was a whole thing." I was rambling; I did that when I was nervous. *Did I just tell a god about my cat's nuts? Oh, someone please save me from myself.*

The two men in the room just looked from me to the cat, who was sitting in the doorway, and back.

"I have no idea what that means, but all right," the real Hades admitted. He looked from Damen to me, then back at the space the cat occupied, scratching his head. Shrugging, he returned his attention to me. "Oracle, I have a little issue I need to discuss with you." His tone was deadly serious. My stomach dropped to my feet at his words, despite the fact that I knew this was coming.

"One Jacob McCabe." The way he spoke his full name sent a shiver down my spine.

I looked to Damen, whose attention was rapt on the god.

"Uh, yes. I know him." One thing my father taught me—well, come to think of it, the *only* thing his drunk ass taught me—other than to never mix gin and vodka, oh and to clean up his messes—was to never admit to anything unless the accuser is direct.

The god narrowed his eyes at me, and I swore the temperature dropped about ten degrees in the room. I began hearing a rapid clicking sound, but after a moment, I realized it was the chattering of my own teeth.

"His soul was due in the River Styx today. Any idea why I'm a soul short?" He leaned forward, his arms resting on his knees.

"Miscounted?" I suggested in an innocent tone.

"Oracle, I have little patience for humans on a good day. Today isn't a good day." There was a clear warning, not only in his words and tone, but in the way his body conveyed the words.

I had to swallow to clear the lump that had formed in my throat.

"I touched him and saw he would die. I couldn't let a little kid die. It was my fault, and Damen had nothing to do with it. So if you have to kill me, then so be it." My eyes burned with unshed tears, and my chest grew tight with the frantic beating of my pounding heart.

"Hades, if I may—" Damen started, but was cut off by a flick of the god's fingers. Damen stood frozen, but still breathing. I just blinked at him. What had he done?

"I know neither he nor his family were on your list, so here is where the problem is." He leaned in, placing his palms flat on the coffee table. "You're new to this power, and new to being the intermediary between the gods and mortals. However, what you've done is broken the rules the gods set on the oracle and the laws of nature."

I knew this was serious. I knew this could be the thing that killed me. But all I kept seeing was Jacob's bouncing red curls lying lifeless on the ground. All I could see was a tragedy I could prevent.

"He was just a child. I saw something I knew was wrong, so I did something about it. How can you really believe his life isn't valuable?" I wasn't trying to anger the gods—well, anger them more than I already had. However, I wanted him to see my side of things.

"Oracle, that isn't something for you to decide. What if he grows up to be the very thing that ends all of mankind? When the downfall of mankind could have been avoided, how will you judge your actions?"

I hadn't thought of it that way. Holy shit! What if I'd doomed the world? I hadn't seen that far into the future. The truth was, I had reacted to what was in front of me, and that's it.

"I-I hadn't really thought of that." I was unable to meet his eyes.

"Oracle, I get a bad reputation for being an evil god. The truth is that death is just as important as creation. We can't have a beginning without something ending. There is a balance that is to be maintained." Everything he was saying made sense. But what I couldn't wrap my head around was why this had to happen to maintain that balance. Why children? Before I could ask, he went on.

"Some things live, and others die. There's no rhyme or reason. That's the job of the Fates. But we must maintain the balance."

"Why?" I asked.

"There's a trickle-down effect. If one life is allowed to be saved, then the balance is gone. If the balance is gone, that will throw the whole world off." It just kept sounding like he was saying the same thing over and over.

"I get it, balance, but what's going to happen?" I knew this was a stupid question, but I needed to know how bad things could get.

"Seventy-nine AD, 1346 to 1353, 1929—all years an oracle decided the laws we'd set upon them were flexible. Pompeii, the black death, the stock market crash on the modern world. The gods will punish the mortals; we will right the wrong you created." He stood up as if to leave.

"I wish I could tell you I was sorry. I wish I could tell you that given what I know now that I'd do something different, but in reality, I likely wouldn't," I admitted.

"I know, oracle. And because of that heart, I will give you two days. On the setting of the second day, if I don't have a soul to replace the one you stole, I will not stop the rest of the gods from raining down upon this land and killing everyone in it. I want a soul. One that's given freely. Or the soul of the child. Either will do."

"Take mine!" I blurted out with no thought as I stood to my feet. If I had to sacrifice myself for this town I now called home, I would.

The tall man turned, walked up to me, and cupped my face. His skin was warm, nearing hot. It was like he was running one hell of a fever.

"Oracle, it's not your time to die. Besides, I like you. I'm not ready to see your soul." He ran his thumb along my cheek, leaving overheated skin in his wake.

Glancing over to where the frozen Damen stood, he smiled menacingly.

"Too bad that brute got to you first. I tried to tell Zeus the line of Hercules would be too much, but hey, who listens to the master of Hell?" Did he just make a joke? He looked at me expectantly, like he was waiting on me to laugh.

Shrugging, he snapped his fingers.

"—interject for just a moment," Damen sputtered as he blinked, looking around. Frowning, he huffed, "Where'd he go?"

Then it was my turn to look around. He was gone.

"He left, I guess." I walked to the front door. I let my head fall lightly to the hard wood. Just what in hell was I going to do?

I could feel Damen's body against my back, his warmth easing the knot in my stomach slightly.

"What happened, Lana?" I didn't want to tell him, mostly because I didn't want him to do what I knew he would—offer up himself. However, keeping it from him felt dishonest, and I didn't want to start whatever was blooming between us on a lie.

Taking a deep breath, I turned around, and caged in his arms, I told him everything Hades had told me.

Neither of us spoke for a long moment. We just stood there, looking at one another. I studied every feature on his face. I let my eyes make memories of every freckle, the rich colors of his eyes, and the small scar that disrupted the dark brown of his left eyebrow. I had no idea why, but it seemed like this was the right choice in the moment, knowing him.

"Well, oracle, what do we do?" He rubbed his hands down my arms.

"I don't know."

It was the truth. It wasn't like I could go out and pick some poor shmuck up and kill them. This had to be someone who knew what would happen. It had to be someone who wanted to die.

"I could offer myself . . ." he offered, like I knew he would.

My chest hurt at the thought of losing him. I would never let that happen, but how could I stop it? How could I stop the wrath of the gods from raining down?

"We have two days to figure this out, right?"

I nodded as a yawn slipped out.

"Then let's go to bed and make a plan in the morning." He pulled me into his arms. I didn't want to take comfort in his embrace. I felt like I didn't deserve it. I'd gotten us in this mess, and I had to figure out a way to get us out of it.

Climbing into the bed, I let myself sink into his body. I wish I could say I fell into a contented dreamless sleep, but that wasn't at all what happened. Rather, I found sleeping to be a fruitless venture. I did, however, formulate a plan. Hades said they wouldn't take my soul, but what if they had to? There were no more females left in my family. The oracle would die with me. It was a shit plan, but I saw no other options.

CHAPTER 10

"*A*re you one hundred percent sure that murder is completely off the table?" Damen raised an eyebrow as he garbled the question around a massive bite of bagel.

Rubbing the bridge of my nose, I glared at him and sighed. "Yeah, pretty darn sure."

"Just checking," he replied defensively.

I knew he was trying to lighten the mood, but I was so stressed trying to figure out this whole mess, nothing really helped.

I searched the whole journal my ya-ya had left me, looking for anything she'd written that could help, but found nothing.

Letting my head fall forward, I lightly banged my forehead on the table. I let out a loud groan and flung my arms over my head.

"Lana," Damen called. I ignored him.

I felt his strong hand on the back of my neck rubbing circles. I wanted to just get my happy ass back into that room, strip the two of us down, and curl up and forget everything going on.

"We could leave." I breathed the thought, and somehow once the words had left my lips, I wished I could take them back.

"Lana, you know—"

"I know," I agreed, cutting him off. "We can't run from this, I know. I just have no idea what to do." Finally, I lifted my head up.

"I guess the Fates will always get their due." His words seemed to have a haunting tone to them. But there was something in them that caused my head to tilt to the side.

"Say that again?" The world stopped spinning for a single moment, and everything shrank to a single pin prick.

"The Fates, they always get their due?" He observed, though it came out more as a question this time, but then it hit me. The Fates. The three Fates.

"The Fates!" I screamed as I stood up. However, I must have moved too fast, as the momentum sent Damen flying back and then tumbling to the ground.

"Damn, sorry," I hurried, offering him a hand. While he took it, I knew he didn't need to.

"The Fates. You know the three Fates. What if we found them? What is the superstition? Find the Fates and they grant you a boon, right? That's what Ray said." My thoughts were scattered as the words fell rapid-fire from my lips.

"Uh, isn't that a genie and the lamp thing? Not sure how accurate that story is." He raised an eyebrow.

Shaking my head, I bolted up and out of the kitchen. I ran into the living room, past a confused-looking Hades, over to the bookshelf. I started rifling through the hundreds of books that lined the wall. If I glanced at a cover that wasn't what I was looking for, I tossed it over my shoulder and moved on. I knew I saw this damn book. Slipping out a red leather book, I glanced at the title, *Greek Architecture: The Base of Modern Plumbing.*

"Nope." I sighed and tossed it.

Hades hissed from somewhere behind me, but I kept on going. As I tossed book after book, I became more and more frantic. Why—

"Ouch!" Damen yelled as I heard a deep thud.

"Sorry, but I know it's here! I saw it!" I tossed three more in quick succession.

I grabbed a black leather-bound book that simply read, *The Fates.*

"I knew I'd seen it!" I nearly screamed, as I plopped to the floor and cracked the book open.

The tome started out with basic info.

"Three sisters, they are the Fates controlling the fates of mankind, they are hags, blah blah blah." This wasn't what I wanted. I was running out of time.

I flipped through the book, reading only about every fourth word, hoping like hell something would jump out at me.

My heart stopped when I saw the words.

"To find the Fates, one must but look to the north and call out their true names. If the speaker of words is deemed worthy, the Fates will reveal themselves posthaste. Though this might sound easy, it's anything but. The Fates are fickle and like to play games. What they say isn't always what will happen, as in the end, the Fates will always get their due," I read aloud.

"What the hell does that mean?" Damen blurted.

I wasn't honestly sure.

"I mean, I guess I just say their names? Then if they want to come, they poof?" It's not like there was an instruction manual for this kind of thing, beyond the book in my hands. The reality was that these books were written by humans who saw the living history of my people as nothing more than a myth. Within each of the pages of every book written, there were a million contradictions, doubts, and lies; then in the spaces between the words was the unknown. The truths that had been all but lost through time. Truths that became myths because we lost ourselves.

"Do you know their names?" he wondered, clearly thinking I didn't. *Oh ye of little faith.*

"I do, actually. But there's really no telling if it would actually work."

Hades strutted into the room tentatively. Likely to be sure he wouldn't be beaned with another book. He stepped onto my lap, turned around, and settled down. As crazy as my cat was, he seemed to know when I needed him.

"Well, what are you waiting for?"

"What if it doesn't work?" I whispered.

"Well, then go back to plan A," he remarked confidently.

"We cannot murder someone!" I sighed, rolling my eyes.

Taking a deep breath, I tried to clear my mind. This had to work because I wasn't sure what else to do. I didn't want to die, but I also didn't want anything to happen to this town.

"Clotho." She was the sister who dispensed the life threads of all mortals. "Lachesis." She was the weaver who was responsible for weaving the threads. "Lachesis." She was the sister who dispensed the threads. "Atropos." She was responsible for cutting the life threads. While together the sisters knew the lives of mortals, they couldn't see beyond their individual tasks.

After I spoke the last sister's name aloud, I wish I could say I felt the air around me change or that I reappeared somewhere else, but nothing. Hades let out a low warning growl, but that wasn't exactly new.

"Fuck!" I spat.

"Oh, she said a cuss word!" a small voice chuckled.

My eyes popped open in surprise. I flew to my feet, causing a seriously pissed off Hades to tumble to the floor.

"Aw, she's so mean to the kitty! Here, kitty kitty!" another voice called out.

Damen whirled around, and his eyes grew wide in alarm. Then I saw what he saw.

Three little girls all dressed alike, scattered throughout the small living space. They wore fluffy pink dresses with a kind of white lace trim. One darted after Hades. One sat on the floor cross-legged, rifling through the books, and the other was jumping on the couch as if it were her own personal trampoline.

"Holy shit, when did this turn into a daycare?" Damen shrieked, eyeing the jumping girl.

"I don't even know what's going on right now." I was completely dazed.

The little girl flipping through the books gazed up at me. She had a full face topped with wisps of featherlight white hair. But it wasn't her pale skin or white hair that caused my very soul to shake. It was her unfocused red eyes.

"Did you not call upon us, oracle?" She had a small angelic voice. Her words were so mature, yet her tone so young. It was so strange.

"Oh, uh, I mean, I called on the Fates?" It came out as a question mostly because this was not at all what I'd expected.

"That's us! We really liked your cat, so that's the reason we came." The one who'd been chasing Hades giggled. She walked into the room cradling the large white cat.

"Oh, be careful. Hades can be pretty temperamental," I warned. That's just what I needed, my damn cat scratching a Fate and then us all dying.

"Oh, kitty loves getting pets!" She laughed while stroking Hades's silky fur. And damn it if the flippin' cat didn't start purring so loudly I could hear it over the squeaks and groans of the poor couch.

"These are them? The three Fates? I thought they were old hags?" Damen wondered in a low tone.

The child on the couch stopped jumping for a moment to yell, "They are old hags! Just look at them!"

"Hey! That's not nice! I'm not a hag. You're a hag!" the one holding Hades spat.

After that, the three broke out into an argument over who was the biggest hag. My jaw pretty much dropped to the ground as my brain couldn't make sense of what my eyes were seeing. They were children, as in, they couldn't be more than a day over eight.

"I had no idea this would be a babysitting job," Damen whispered.

"Yeah, you and me both," I agreed, trying to keep count of just how many kids we had.

I thought this was my only chance to figure out how to get out of this mess, yet here I was with three bickering, er, scratch that, wrestling children. I had no idea what to do with this. I'd never really had any experience with kids, so I was kind of at a loss.

Clearing my throat, I screeched, "Excuse me!"

The three paused mid-arm bar and looked at me.

"I asked you here. Don't I get a wish or boon or something?"

"What do we look like, genies?" the three small voices cried at once.

"Ah, that's what I said!" Damen agreed. I cut him an angry glare, but he only shrugged.

"You're supposed to be on my side," I huffed indignantly. Taking in a deep breath and letting it out slowly, I said, "Listen, I just need your help."

The three untangled themselves, stood, smoothed out their frilly dresses, and looked expectantly at me.

The one on the left curtsied before saying, "Clotho."

Then the one in the middle did a little bow and chortled, "Lachesis."

The last triplet slowly walked around me, seeming to examine me. Once she stood back where she'd started, she added, "Atropos."

Of the three, Atropos was the one who gave me the willies. It was like she was looking for something only she could see, her eerie red eyes not really focusing on me, but somehow seeing through me.

"No one ever calls us to help them," Clotho whined.

"Yeah, they just call us to complain," Lachesis huffed as she crossed her tiny arms over her chest.

"Or to bring back the dead," Atropos added in a haunting tone. A shiver ran up my spine, causing me to shudder.

"Oh, I'm sorry. I guess I, um, messed up, kind of. Well, I mean, no, I totally messed up. I'm rambling. Let me start over." I couldn't seem to get my words to come out in any order that made any damn sense.

"Jacob. He's just a little thing. A baby really. It was my fault. I touched him and saw he was going to die. I saved him even though he wasn't on the petitioner list." My words were rushed and my throat tight with stifled emotion.

"Ah, yes. Hades was due a soul, yet when I tried to cut his life string, it would not cut. I thought it most odd." Atropos seemed to reminisce, her vacant red eyes staring at me all the while.

"Oh, I know he's mad!" Lachesis giggled.

"He said he either needs Jacob's soul or one given up freely. I want you to cut my thread," I instructed firmly.

"Uh, how about hell no!" Damen interrupted, like I knew he would.

"Shh," Lachesis snapped at him.

"Let her speak. I'm intrigued," Clotho ordered.

"I will allow you to cut my thread, leaving the human's will up to you, as I am the end of my line." I'd known from the moment I called upon the Fates that this would be my offer. The Fates had always hated the oracle. They saw the power of foresight to be in direct competition with their own divinity.

"Hmm, interesting indeed, sisters. We've never liked the powers the oracle was granted," Clotho said.

Damen grabbed my upper arm and pulled me to him.

"You can't do this. I won't let you. If you die, I die. Our fates are tied." I could hear the strain in his voice.

"But if you die, I don't." This time it was my voice that cracked.

"I have your thread, oracle. Would you like to see it? See your past?" The Fate's words caused me to whirl around.

"No," I whispered without thinking. I didn't need to see it. I'd lived it.

"What about Jensen's?" My heart nearly stopped at her words.

The Fate reached out in the air and seemed to pluck something. Drawing her pinched fingers back, she withdrew a long silver thread from nothing. The string seemed to glitter in the light as if made of liquid diamonds.

A twinkle of light caught my eye. It was Jensen's smiling face, and it caused my heart to hurt.

I felt a small hand cup my face as a heated tear tracked down my cheek.

"Oh, young one, you have so much living to do. As much as we would love to end the oracle, the gift no human should ever have, this isn't willing."

My heart sank at her words, mostly because she was right. I didn't want to die. But then we were back at square one.

"And guardian, don't think to volunteer. You have her to live for," Atropos added, a warning in her tone.

"I don't know what to do," I whispered, unable to trust my own emotions. My knees gave out, and I collapsed on my ass to the floor. "All of this because I forgot to put gloves on."

Clotho walked over and sat down next to me.

"Look, child, I want to show you something." I almost laughed at her calling me a child, but I went with it.

She pressed her forefinger and thumb together and then gently rubbed them back and forth. At first nothing happened, then a tiny light began to glow. It was faint at first, but soon it grew to nearly blinding. It was the most beautiful thing I'd ever seen. I could feel the life within it, feel the soul shining like a beacon. It seemed to cry out to my own soul. Suddenly, she stopped, but the light was still there. Now it glowed on its own.

She took her other hand and pinched the tiny spark and drew it out. There was a glittering thread, just like Jensen's had been.

"This is the birth of a soul," she marveled, her own voice filled with awe.

A moment later, her sister walked over and plucked it from her as if it were a ripe plum.

Lachesis ran her fingers along the thread of this new life while smiling and nodding. She then began making intricate knots along it.

"These are moments. Some may come to be; some may not. They may change; they may not, but this has potential." Her fingers flew along the string so fast I had trouble tracking them. Once she was done, she walked over to Atropos and handed her the new thread.

Atropos took the soul and inspected it thoughtfully. While her eyes didn't track along the thread in a way I could understand, I knew she could see the soul in her own way.

She took out a pair of what looked like well-worn shears.

While looking at me, she spoke, "Only I know the moment of death. This isn't out of hate, out of love, or out of predestination. It is because nothing in the mortal world is infinite. All things are born, and all things die." Then, near the top of the thread, she let the scissors hover.

"Wait! It's just a child, a baby!" I cried, lurching forward.

She cut the thread, leaving barely a half an inch between her fingers, and sending the rest to the floor. I fell to my knees, cradling the faded soul in my hands.

"Why?" I cried.

Atropos leaned down and cupped my face, and for once it seemed as if she really saw me.

"Child, weep not for the life that wasn't, but rather for the life that was lived and the love that was received." She offered me her hand. In it was the still glowing scrap of the soul that had just been woven.

"Send the soul to Hades, oracle. It's a privilege to do so," she instructed. I took the thread from her hand as if it were a precious and fragile doll. In a way, it was.

"What do I do now?" I whispered.

"Don't you know, child? Let your power guide you."

Taking a deep breath, I closed my eyes and focused on the feel of the barely there thread. I felt so stupid. I had no idea what I was doing, but then again, that had always been the case. I'd never known what I was doing, my whole life.

My mother had left when I was a kid, leaving me with my alcoholic father. When she died, I felt the same as I'd always felt—confused and lost. Even with dating and school, I'd never known what I was doing.

Opening my eyes, I sighed. "I don't know what I'm doing. I've never known what I was doing."

"You've lost trust in yourself. Trust your power and you'll see a clear path." Her voice was soft and soothing.

She was right. I closed my eyes and let go. Instead of looking for the answer, I let go of everything. Then the path was clear.

I raised my open palm to my lips and let out a long breath, blowing the tiny soul into the air. It fluttered for a few moments before floating off and disappearing. I knew it was on its way to where it was supposed to go. I knew this deep within my own soul.

"But why children?" My question was nothing more than a breath, but I knew they'd heard it.

"Because all things end. No matter the age or time, they all must end," Lachesis answered.

"So what do I do now? Hades needs a soul. One that must be freely given, or the child's soul. I can't just go out and ask someone for their soul."

"You can, though." The male voice came from behind me. I whirled around to face my father, who stood in the doorway.

Damen walked over to him, blocking his view of me.

"I have no idea how you got in here, or why. But I really don't care. My whole purpose is to protect the oracle. I'm going to need you to go before —"

He paused as I walked up and placed a calming hand on his shoulder.

"Damen, it's okay. That's my dad." Damen's back stiffened at my words. I'd told him about my past, but only barely. After a long drawn-out moment, Damen moved to the side.

There stood the man I'd not seen in close to five years. He looked so much older than I remembered. His whole body looked sickly, yellow even. It was likely all the years of drinking he'd done.

"Why are you here, Dad?" I narrowed my eyes, not inviting him in. How in the hell he'd even found this place with the wards up was beyond me.

"Your grandmother wrote me a letter and told me to come here at this time today. She said you needed me. She also included this pendant." He pointed to his chest. My guess was that was how he actually found the place.

"Okay, why now? What did her letter say?" Part of me felt so betrayed that my ya-ya had known this would happen, yet didn't warn me.

"Could I come in?" He was looking past me to Damen. For once he didn't seem drunk. He didn't seem angry. He just looked like a normal guy, which in itself was abnormal.

I nodded and moved aside.

The three Fates eyed my father with great interest.

There we all sat in my tiny living room. The sacred oracle, my guardian, the three Fates, and my dad, all surrounded by creepy-ass dolls. If this day got any stranger, I might actually combust. Oh, and the cat, the crazy-ass feline who kept darting in and out, his bouncing balls a testament to his greatness.

"Would anyone like any tea?" one of the Fates bubbled. I had no idea who was who anymore.

"Tea? You can make tea?" Damen asked in a confused tone.

"Yes, boy. I'm a Fate, not an imbecile." She huffed as the three walked into the kitchen.

"Dad, why are you here?" I asked again, just trying to make sense of it all.

He fidgeted for a moment, looking uncomfortable. A strained silence fell over us as we waited for him to say whatever it was he was going to say.

"I stopped drinking about a year ago, after I found out I was going into liver failure. I've been on the transplant list, but the reality is, because of my past, I'll likely never get one."

I shouldn't care. I shouldn't give a single damn about the man who'd put me through hell, but I couldn't seem to make myself not care. I said nothing as I felt Damen's hand slip into mine.

"When I got your grandmother's letter, I knew I had to come. She said you'd have need of me. And after hearing what I just heard, I'm here to help you. I want to give up my soul for the little boy's." The world stopped turning, and everything but him and me seemed to fall away.

My whole world shrank to this moment, to those words. All I could hear after this was the beating of my own heart in my ears.

"Why?" was the only word I could manage to get out.

"I've done nothing my whole life. Wasted every chance I've ever been given. You were the only good thing ever did, and even that I found a way to mess up. When your mom left, I was given a chance to be the dad you needed, and I failed. When she died, I was once again given a chance, and yet again I failed. Here I am, but this time—" He paused and looked at me fully. Our matching eyes met and locked.

"This time I won't give up my chance to do the only good thing I've ever done."

He was serious.

"No." I couldn't even believe the word came out so firmly. I guess there was still a large part of me that wanted to believe in her daddy, that wanted to be loved by him. If he did this, I'd never get that chance.

"Tea?" one of the Fates called from the doorway.

My dad stood up nervously.

"I'm willing to give my soul in place of the little boy's. Freely given." His voice didn't even tremble.

"No." It was weak, but I spoke anyway.

"How very interesting," one of the fates mused. I thought this one was Clotho.

"Indeed, Clotho. Thoughts on him, Atropos? In the end, it's your choice if it will suffice," Lachesis said.

Atropos scooped up a still-purring Hades and walked up to my dad. She pursed her lips and began to walk a tight circle around him. She then handed Hades to my father, picked up the thread, and ran her small fingers along it. Her brow pinched and furrowed, and her bowed lips pulled taut as she inspected the thread.

"You can't be serious!" I tried to cross the small space to stop her, but felt two strong arms cage around me.

"Damen, let me go!" I ordered as I thrashed against him. He only squeezed me tighter.

"I'm so sorry." His whispered words did nothing to ease my concern.

"Don't. Do. This. Damen. Please!" I begged as my vision blurred with tears.

"I'm so, so sorry," he chanted over and over.

"This is my only chance at a dad, a real dad!" I screamed. That caused the Fate to look from me to my dad and back again.

Grabbing the cat from my father, she set Hades on the floor and patted him on his rump as if to say, "Move along." She then plucked out my father's thread fully for everyone to see. It didn't shine at all. In the middle it was worn, dark, and tattered, except for the barest bit at the end.

"His soul will do," she determined.

"Wait! Just wait!" This couldn't be happening! This was my mistake. One thing I'd done caused all of this. I should be the one to pay, no one else.

My father walked over to me, but looked at Damen, whom I was still fighting to escape.

"You take care of her. You hear me? You take care of her like I should have." His voice was raw, filled with pain. It was such an emotion-filled plea, I couldn't help but sob at it.

"Why wait until now? *Why?*" I screamed. My throat burned, but nothing mattered.

"Better late than never?" he joked half-heartedly. That only caused me to sob harder.

Cupping my cheek, he smiled softly. That smile I recalled seeing only a few times in my childhood, that smile I used to dream of getting to see again.

"Oh, peanut. I've done nothing in my life I could be proud of, aside from you. If this is the last and only thing I can do for you to be a good father, then please let me do it." With that, he turned his back on me and walked toward the Fate.

"I won't ask if you're ready for death, for no one should be," Atropos said.

He nodded and looked over to me.

She took out her shears once more and lifted them over the thread.

"Love you, peanut. Wish I could have been better." He choked as tears rolled down his cheek.

"DAD!" I was sobbing and thrashing. I tried like hell to stop this, but Damen wouldn't let me go.

"I love y—" He dropped to the floor in a heap.

My eyes flew to the fate who still held his life thread, except the glowing end had been cut and laid on the ground, fading.

I let out a scream that I'd only ever heard once, once in a vision of loss. Aster's scream of loss, the one that surely could have been heard by the gods, was really my own.

Finally, after I had no more voice, Damen let me go. I fell to the floor and scrambled over to the lifeless body that once housed the soul of my father.

They all just stood around me as I sobbed. I cried for a man I wished I could have known in the end, but mostly I cried for the little girl who still wanted her daddy, who wished he could have been the man he should have always been.

"Come, oracle, send him on his way home," Atropos whispered softly.

How could I be expected to do this? I didn't move at first. I sat there staring at the tattered thread.

Despite my tears and pain, I held out my hand as she dropped his thread into it. It felt heavy and warm. Unlike the last one, I could feel how worn the soul had been.

I took in a deep breath, but didn't let it out. If I let it out, I knew it would be like saying goodbye, something I wasn't sure I was ready for.

"Go on. Goodbye doesn't always mean the end." It was Damen's words that allowed me to exhale my father's soul to the underworld.

Suddenly, I felt hollow and raw. I just sat there and cried. I cried for the mistake I'd made and the sacrifice that was given. I cried and cried. I cried until I ran out of tears.

Between sobs I remembered the Fates telling Damen they would take care of everything in the house, but then they would have to leave.

Setting me in the bed, Damen kissed my head.

"I'm so sorry. I know you'll hate me. I hope someday you'll forgive me." His words were so full of heartache, it caused a tightening in my chest.

I wanted to hate him. It would be easier to blame him, hell, blame someone. But the truth was I could only blame myself.

"We have a lot of years for you to forgive me. I don't mind waiting. You're worth it," he added as he got off the bed.

"Damen!" I hurried. "Please don't go."

He stopped, his hand on the doorknob. He didn't turn, though.

"Damen, I don't blame you, and I don't hate you. Please don't let me sleep alone." The words burned my raw throat.

He opened the door and walked out. I'd never felt so alone in my life as I did in that moment. I had nothing, I had—

The door swung open, and Damen stood there in his silk boxer shorts that sported tiny flamingos.

"Just had to go get pretty for you," he joked as he heaved his big body over the small space and jumped on the bed.

"That wasn't nice," I chided, but my heart wasn't in it.

He only smiled and pulled me into his arms. Though my wounds were still fresh and raw, for once, I allowed myself to take comfort in him. In his arms, I felt safe and protected. I was finally able to release the breath it felt like I'd been holding for years. And just like that, I slid into a deep sleep.

CHAPTER 11

our months later

"By Hades's bouncing balls is it cold!" I shivered between clattering teeth. I swear I could see my breath freeze and fall to the ground.

"Yeah, well, you were the one who wanted to come out and do the hot cocoa and cookie thing, so you have no one to blame but your stomach." Damen pulled me in tighter to him.

"Hey, at least now when I wear gloves everywhere, no one thinks I'm batshit."

"I wouldn't go that far, oracle." He laughed at his own joke.

"Ha. Ha. So very funny. No, really, you should be a comedian, guardian. I could be your manager," I joked in a robotic tone.

"Cute," he whispered as he slid a finger under my chin. Pinching me lightly, he dipped his lips to mine. Heat started from my mouth and spread like a wildfire to the rest of my body. What started as a chaste expression grew to something more serious.

Before things got too out of hand, I broke away from his teasing tongue.

Out of breath, he flirted, "I know how to warm you up."

"That you do, but this is a family event, and well, cookies," I chattered in a dreamy tone.

"Oh, I see where I stand," he grumbled, though I knew his heart wasn't in it.

"Yup, it goes Hades, cookies, then you," I explained, unable to hide my smile.

We spent the next hour wandering around town, sipping hot chocolate and nibbling on cookies. If I thought the town was magical in August, nothing could compare to December. I'd never really lived somewhere with so much snow. So I thought when it got cold, people hid inside by the fire. I couldn't have been more wrong. The whole town seemed to come alive, as though they were hibernating in the summer, waiting for the first snowfall to wake.

I didn't know it was possible to fall in love with a place, but that's just what happened. I was totally in love with Havenwood Falls.

"My superhero!" a little boy screeched in a pitch I honestly didn't know was possible. I turned to see a bright red streak dart right at Damen. And just like I knew he would, he scooped Jacob up into his arms.

"Hey, little man!" Damen cooed as he held the boy.

"Hey, honey! Where's your aunt? I don't want her to worry." I looked around.

"Over there." He pointed over Damen's shoulder.

I looked over, and Aster waved and mouthed, "Sorry!"

"We're good!" I grinned and waved reassuringly.

"You're Lana?" He giggled, looking at me. I couldn't actually recall if he'd ever known my name.

"Yup!" I affirmed with a smile.

"Thank you."

I frowned at his words, not understanding what he was thanking me for.

"For what, honey?"

He wiggled and moved in Damen's arms, causing him to put the boy down.

He stepped over to me and grabbed my hands. He pulled down slightly, so I knelt down until we were on more of the same level.

His little cheeks were tinged red from the cold, making his dark freckles stand out even more. While his face was framed with his green hood, his wild red hair stuck out every which way. He really was a cute thing.

"For your daddy. He's a nice man." He then giggled and ran back to his aunt, waving back all the way.

I couldn't seem to make my legs work. I just stayed there like a statue, frozen on my knees.

"Lana?" Damen asked, helping me to my feet.

He searched my eyes. Clearly, he hadn't heard what Jacob said. I just stared after the little boy as he grabbed a cookie and did a little spin on the sidewalk.

Blinking tears away, I smiled up at my guardian.

"He was a good man," I choked, trying to keep my emotions at bay.

"Who was?" he questioned in a confused tone.

"My dad. In the end, anyway." For the first time in four months it felt easier to breathe. And like I had a hundred times before, I let out a breath, but this time I let everything go. All of the blame, the guilt, all of it.

"There you are." Damen breathed his own sigh of relief.

"What?" I asked, blinking away the snowflakes that had fallen on my eyelashes.

"The real you," he whispered before kissing me.

Breaking the kiss, I smiled warmly at him.

"But there's more cookies." I giggled.

Holding me tighter, he slid a hand to the back of my head, tanking his fingers in my dark hair.

"Come on, oracle, let's go get cookies."

Ah, the way to my heart: cookies. He knew just the right things to say.

"Oh, and cocoa, too," he added with a wink. All I could do was laugh.

~

We hope you enjoyed this story in the Havenwood Falls series featuring a variety of supernatural creatures. The series is a collaborative effort by multiple authors.

Books in the main Havenwood Falls series you might also enjoy:

Forget You Not by Kristie Cook
Alpha's Queen by Lila Felix
Ink & Fire by R.K. Ryals
Affliction Mine by C.J. Pinard
A Demon's Redemption by JD Nelson

Also look for the YA line, Havenwood Falls High; the historical paranormal line, Legends of Havenwood Falls; the sexier side of town, Havenwood Falls Sin & Silk; the local supernatural college, Sun & Moon Academy; and the Havenwood Falls holiday short story anthologies.

Stay up to date at www.HavenwoodFalls.com

ABOUT THE AUTHOR

Emily Cyr is a stay-at-home mom turned writer. She holds a degree in middle grades education with certification in English and social science. She has always had a love of all things paranormal and fantasy, but it wasn't until Emily's husband said the words, "Why not?" that she considered putting her thoughts and ideas into the book, *The Lightning Prophecy*. This trilogy was just the start for Emily. It seemed to open a creative door that had been locked.

Emily has always been an avid reader. Through reading came her love of writing. The more she read, the more she knew she wanted to create her own world. Many of her first works were fan fiction.

Emily and her family currently reside in San Antonio, Texas. She has an incredibly supportive husband, who is also an officer in the United States Air Force. They have three sons, ages 8, 7, and 3. Somehow, even with the demands of being a parent to three little boys, she finds time to escape to her fantasies and write them down.

Currently, Emily has two urban fantasy series out, but stay tuned via her website, www.EmilyCyr.com, for more!

Play list for *Fate's Demand*:
    Juice - Lizzo
    Like a Girl - Lizzo
    Beauty Marks - Ciara
    Almost - Hozier
    Movement - Hozier
    No Plan - Hozier

Cool Blue Reason - Cake
My Boy - Billie Eilish
Ocean Eyes - Billie Eilish
You Are the Reason - Calum Scott

AN EXCERPT

A Havenwood Falls New Adult Novella

HAVENWOOD FALLS

THE WU AND THE WAND

T.V. HAHN

The Wu & the Wand (A Havenwood Falls Novella) by T.V. Hahn

In this sequel to *The Winged & the Wicked* and *The Ward & the Wanderers,* the spring fae's family is in trouble again in another Teeny Weeny fairy tale.

Relentlessly trying to get back to her simple Havenwood Falls life, Teeny Weeny Tahini enjoys nothing more than her morning teas at the Broastful Brew with Mayor Barbie Stuart. But that seems to be where she always is whenever trouble comes into her life. This time it's a tantalizing Asian gentleman, a world-famous professional gamer who's wooed the local teens. But is tantalizing the right word? Mr. Wu has all of Teeny's senses on full alert.

When her friend Nina—the woman she hopes her nephew will propose to—suddenly disappears, Teeny is certain Mr. Wu has the answers. She never expects what she learns, though, and now it's up to her to save not only Havenwood Falls, but an entire dynasty of another place and another time. But first she must master her father's wand she'd recently found—and figure out her feelings for the Wu.

THE WU & THE WAND

BY T.V. HAHN

The bedroom chamber was still as night, though it was only slightly darkened by the oncoming twilight. Four people were in the chamber: the young boy (the poor soul who brought us all here in the first place, or so we thought), his mother, his father, and myself.

A straw of hay rustled across the rice paper floor. That was the only sound that could be heard for what seemed an eternity, until the stillness was interrupted with the eerie raspy rattle of death emitting from the frail body, of whom we stood by the bedside. His skin was waxen and yellow, and so chilled to touch that it numbed one's fingers.

The child had not moved for what felt like a century, but was most likely two or three days. Not a single movement could be detected underneath his sleeping eyelids. That at least might have given us an indication that he was still aware . . . maybe still with us.

Suddenly, the booming command came: "YOU MUST CURE HIM!"

Regardless of the strength of the command, it was easy to discern that it contained worry and grief, and even more—concern for the future of our world.

"Your Highness," I spoke slowly, trying very carefully to phrase the rest of my response so as not to anger but to do my job, "this is no illness I am familiar with." I paused.

"WHY ARE YOU HERE, THEN, IF YOU CANNOT CURE HIM? YOU SHALL BE EXECUTED AT SUNRISE FOR YOUR INSOLENCE AND DECEIT!"

"Your Highness, I am not speaking from either insolence or deceit. There is another force that is upon us. I don't believe this is an illness, but a curse. Someone or something does not want the young prince to survive." And then I bowed my entire body as low to the floor as I could possibly flatten myself.

It must have worked, because fortunately the ruler wavered. It was evident that the poor child had become afflicted too quickly and with no rhyme or reason for its onset. A curse may very well have been the cause.

"WHAT DO YOU NEED?"

"Your Highness, I need time"—the ruler lifted his staff, indicating he had heard enough, but I continued as quickly as I could—"which, of course, I am keenly aware that we do not have. But I have a method of overcoming that." I prayed under my breath. "My devotion and divination with Spirit Crane has put me in good standing with the spirit, and I believe She will assist me in finding out who placed the curse, and, to that end, how to break it!"

The rulers, having reigned so long and becoming so arrogant as such royalty tended to do, had lost their touch with the people. The child prince, however, was blessed with the knowledge and the gifts of his ancestors, and the people loved him. I loved him.

If he died, the people would revolt against not only the rulers, but the mysteries of mankind, and this realm would dissolve into shreds of nothingness.

But that was not my only challenge. I loved him, and I loved my people, but I loved this world too. I wanted—I *needed*—it to survive. There was something very dark, dangerous, and deadly out there, and I needed to use everything in my powers to find it and eradicate it.

～

TEENY WEENY

It was another perfectly crisp October morning. I absolutely loved this time of year. It was invigorating. The harvest of all the delicious squashes—pumpkins, crooknecks, hubbards, and the like—had come in. There was such an array of colors upon us—the orange maples, the golden-leafed aspens, and of course all of the luxurious evergreens, from the bristlecone pines to the elegant spruces—all of them emitting a fragrance that I could feel.

Havenwood Falls, this small frontier-like town nestled in the cradle of a canyon and cloaked with the mystery of supernaturals and humans cautiously, carefully coexisting, was at its autumn peak, ready to burst with harvest and a few chills and thrills for the Halloweeners.

I grabbed my wool scarf, the latest one given to me by my nephew Mat and his girlfriend Nina, and headed out for my regular rendezvous with my best friend, Barbie a.k.a. Mayor Stuart.

Ah, Mat was not really my nephew, but a cousin. However, with hundreds of years between us, he had always known me as Aunt Siobhan.

My townhome, which housed my palm-reading salon, opened up to the south entrance of the square. I crossed over Main Street, and since we started our rendezvous fairly early in the morning, it was an easy crossing with no traffic. Town Square Park was accentuated with a fountain in its center. Some modern-day folks didn't believe the story that it was rimmed with real gold flakes that spilled from the floors of the gold-traders, some of whom founded this Havenwood Falls in the first place long ago during the gold rush. I was there, so I knew it was true.

As I approached the Broastful Brew, I could already see the mayor sitting at our familiar table.

The Broastful Brew was more of an artifact, kind of like me, than the best coffee shop in Havenwood Falls. Mabel, the owner and operator, landed in Havenwood Falls maybe twenty or thirty years ago. She was perfectly human, if there was such a thing, but that was what she was. I didn't know if she was one of those souls that were actually summoned to come, or if she just came here by happenstance. I suspected the latter. But you never knew.

The tinkle of the shopkeeper's bell rang a simple chime as I opened the door to the Brew. The flowery scent of Dragon Well green tea smacked me so hard in the face that my fingertips started to tingle, as did the tips of my toes. A distinguished Asian fellow lifted his head from the steaming cup of green tea, noting my entrance. He was very handsome with a neatly trimmed Fu Manchu and dark eyes that seemed nearly black. He appeared to be around my age, my glamour age anyway, but it was hard to tell, especially since I sensed in his eyes something much older, ancient even. I felt he may have been an old soul, reincarnated many times.

I nodded at him, hoping he would accept the greeting, and not think of me as too rude for my intense observance of him, then hurried to the back of the Broastful Brew to join the mayor.

"Good morning, Barbie! Boy, that Manchurian tea still has my fingers and toes tingling!"

"Good morning yourself! Are you sure it's that tea making you tingle?" Barbie winked at me and continued, "You were certainly examining that man up and down. He's really quite handsome, don't you think?"

I sat down, then leaned over the table as far as my four-foot-five frame would allow. Barbie obliged and leaned over her side of the table, meeting me more than halfway, her lemon chiffon bouffant bouncing on the top of my head.

"Who is that chap? Looks can be deceiving, you know, especially in Havenwood Falls," I said in a whisper.

"Don't I know it! Look at us! You have more power in your right pinky fingernail than I do from my heel to the top of my beehive. But anyway, that's Tim Wu, Dr. Wu. The Court invited him all the way from China. Don't you remember the discussion?"

"Well, sort of . . . He's some kind of a professional gamer, right? Well, that sounds pretty much like a professional gambler who already lost a couple of letters. I kind of tuned the whole thing out."

"He's more than just a professional gamer, though all the kids in town are excited about the Grand Master being here because of that. He's also a game developer, and his newest game *Rage of Realms* has an interesting premise—dark forces trying to destroy all magic. The Court felt we may be able to glean something from him."

Then the mayor abruptly straightened up in her chair and said, "That reminds me! Siobhan, you really have to consider being on the faculty of the Academy's College of Guardians. Adelaide is teaching one of the potions classes right now, and you know she's probably not the best choice for that subject. Not compared to you. We need you desperately!"

"I really don't think so, Barbie. I'm no teacher. Even after hundreds of years, I feel I am still a student myself, bumbling around this mysterious world."

My nephew Mat came to the table, carrying my usual chamomile tea. He'd been working morning shifts at the Broastful Brew pretty much since he arrived here two years ago.

"Good morning Mayor, Madame Tahini." He winked at me. *What's with all this winking this morning?*

Mat set down the teapot, steeper, and cup, and no sooner did he leave than the Asian gentleman approached the table.

"Good morning, ladies. I hope I'm not interrupting." He spoke in a smooth voice, but his accent seemed out of place, more British. Maybe he grew up in Hong Kong?

"Dr. Wu! A pleasure to see you this morning. Are your quarters comfortable?" the mayor greeted him, then turned to me. "Our guest is staying in one of the cabins at Whisper Falls Inn."

"And who is this charming little woman with you, Mayor?" Dr. Wu asked.

"I'm sorry. I've forgotten my manners! Dr. Timothy Wu, this is Teeny Weeny Tahini, I mean Madame Tahini, our resident palm reader and healer."

"Enchanted to meet you, Madame Tahini. I've dabbled a bit in healing divination myself. It would be a pleasure to share a spot of tea with you sometime, if you would care to join me."

Oh, dear. The tingling sensation started again, and this time it wasn't the tea, and wasn't just my fingers and toes—it extended to my earlobes, the back of my neck, even my nose!

"I would be delighted," I responded, not having any idea where that came from.

"How about four o'clock tomorrow afternoon? I'll meet you at the inn?"

"Oh, uh, four o'clock . . . tomorrow?" I stammered, trying to backtrack now and regain my composure.

"She'll be there!" the mayor piped in, giving me no room to renege.

"Brilliant! I will see you then." Dr. Wu nodded a goodbye and left.

The bell dangling from the front door tinkled again as the esteemed *doctor* left the shop.

Mat returned to the table and asked if we needed anything else. The mayor requested another cup of coffee, but I was still bouncing my tea steeper in my pot, trying to make heads or tails of what had just occurred.

"By the way, Aunt Siobhan, I'd like to show you the gift I got Nina for our second anniversary. I'll come by after my shift is over?"

Mat meant the second anniversary of their meeting and dating. It was a very slow romance in the making. Mostly because Nina, a very talented Italian tailor, was still quite gun shy because of the death of her lover many years ago.

"That'll be fine, Mat. I'll be home."

The mayor got up from the table and bade me farewell, again asking me to consider the Sun and Moon Academy's new College of Supernatural Guardians. I just shook my head. She was persistent, part of the great politician in her.

I finished my tea in solitude, swirling the brew in my cup and wondering what the tea leaves would be telling me about the town's new guest.

Purchase *The Wu & the Wand* where books are sold.

www.ingramcontent.com/pod-product-compliance
Lightning Source LLC
Chambersburg PA
CBHW052007170626
46808CB00007B/2818